THE ADVEN
TARUM MON

The Sphere of Time

Copyright © 2024 Stephen F. Black

Published by Rosebud Press

Paperback ISBN: 978-1-0687352-0-2

All rights reserved

No part of this book may be reproduced in any form or by any electronic or mechanical means, including in information storage and retrieval systems, without permission in writing from the author, with the exception of short excerpts used in a review.

Stephen F. Black has asserted their right under the Copyright, Designs and Patents Act 1988 to be identified as the author of this work.

This book is a work of fiction. Names, characters, places and incidents are either products of the author's imagination or are used fictitiously. Any resemblance to actual persons, living or dead, events, or locales is entirely coincidental.

THE ADVENTURES OF TARUM MON

The Sphere of Time

STEPHEN F. BLACK

Dedication

This book would not have been possible without the following people. First, and most importantly, I would like to thank my beautiful wife and best friend Maureen, she is my muse, and her fantastic input helped my story develop, she also made me so proud when she gave birth to our beautiful daughter who we named Miracle. Thanks also go to my wonderful father Keith who helped me; he was my sounding board. Love you, Dad.

Who could forget the rest of my family and friends for helping realise my dream of being a published author by caring and believing in my talent.

There are two more people I need to thank. They are my brilliantly talented illustrator, my cousin Mark Smith; we grew up together and his artistic genius helped bring my world and book art to life, sadly he has now passed.

Please keep an eye out in the story as I have done something special for him, see if you can spot it.

The other person who, although no longer with us, left a never-fading mark of love on our family's hearts and pushed me to follow my dreams is my mother Jo, the bravest and brightest in everything she did right to the end.

Delve into the world of Xexus; there is always more to explore.

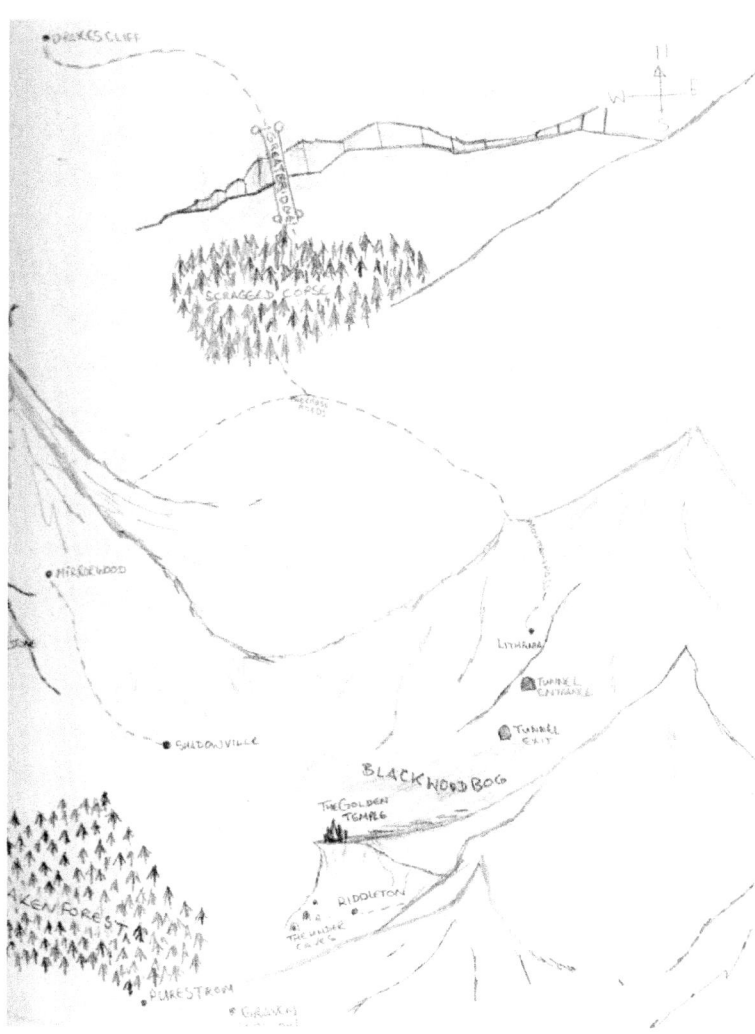

Contents

Dedication 5

The Magic and Seasons of Xexus 11

Prologue 12

Brightleaf Day 1 14

Brightleaf Day 2 24

Brightleaf Day 3 36

Brightleaf Day 4 59

Brightleaf Day 5 82

Brightleaf Day 6 93

Brightleaf Day 7 104

Brightleaf Day 8 124

Brightleaf Day 9 144

Brightleaf Day 10 180

Brightleaf Day 11 198

Epilogue 207

Prologue 209

Bitter Rivals 210

Author Bio 218

ELEMENTAL MAGIC SYMBOLS

 Darc
 Aqua

 Lite
 Poison Magma

 Breeze
 Terrain

The Magic and Seasons of Xexus

The four seasons on Xexus are Brightleaf, Nevern, Broughton and Chillern.

A new year begins after a full circle of seasons. Each book is set in an individual season and helps the story progress.

The magic of Xexus can be found in seven main elemental types, these are: Darc, lite, breeze, aqua, magma, terrain, and poison.

There are also rumours of ancient magics, but so far no one has used them.

All spells sometimes can transform, under the right circumstances, to include more than one element, and this means they will be much more powerful and unpredictable, but this is a rare occurrence.

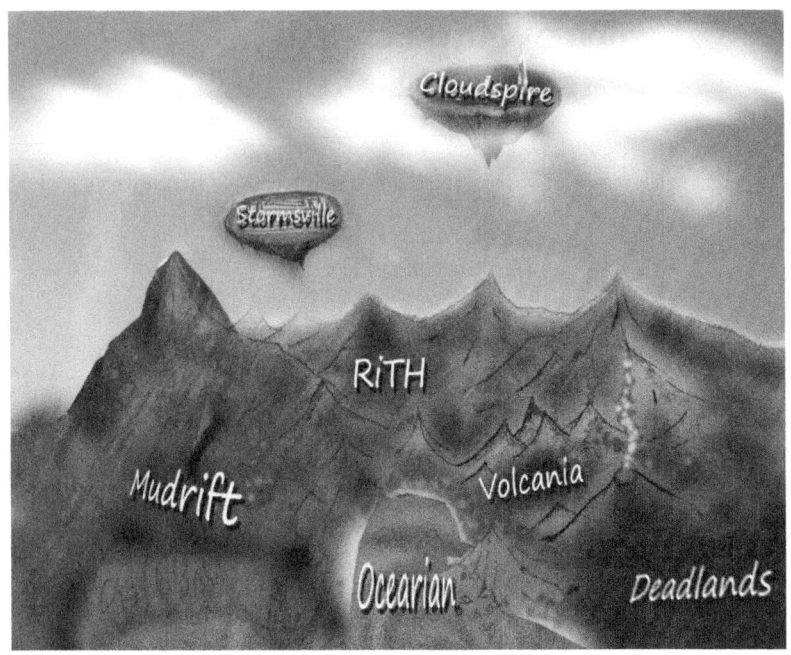

Map of Xexus
Prologue

Welcome adventurers. You are about to discover a vast new world full of mystery, enchantment, and fantasy. This world is known as Xexus.

Xexus was created by a very powerful and magical god called The Magnificent.

Xexus is made up of seven separate continents, collectively they are known as the Joining. Each novel will follow our heroes and reveal its lands and its many beautiful inhabitants and strange creatures.

This story will introduce the continent called:

RITH

Brightleaf Day 1

I would like to invite you into Rith. This continent contains many different races; these include humans, elves, and the occasional troll. It has thick forests bursting with life, bustling towns, and beautiful mythical temples dedicated to their guardian.

Our story begins in a large town called **Drake's Cliff**. Here is where I let our hero tell the story.

Who am I, and what is my part to play? That you will have to wait and see.

It was a typical day in my town, the busy streets were full of traders going about their business, thieves were waiting in the shadows for opportunities, and many warriors and wizards were drinking in the local tavern called **The Moonshine Inn**.

I was busy at our training ground known locally as **Resa's Lea**. After eighteen cycles, which you humans know as years, I was finally an adult.

My name is Tarum; my full name is Tarum Mon. My second name means a lot in our town, as it is connected to two great heroes; my parents.

Their story may surprise you as much as it surprises me because, no matter who I ask in the town, including our leader, no one will tell me anything about them. Anyway, enough grumbling, now a little about me. I have a medium build, short, blonde hair, and light blue eyes, which is common of my elven race. My current job is as an assistant to our leader Resa De Montess.

She is a formidable and fair leader. If I were to guess, she is probably in her late fifties, not that I am brave enough to tell her that. She is a powerful sorceress and wears a rune-covered cloak, and through her many travels and years of training, she is now adept at all elemental magic.

She seems to have a secret, though. I notice her, on the odd occasion, looking far away and muttering about her own continent, **Volcania**, and in her tent, she has a drawer that she seems to open a lot. I have no idea what it contains, but I know she left her homeland many years ago to take position as our leader, when our old commander passed away; apparently, she was very good friends with him.

After many years of training and a natural ability to learn, I am both a skilled mage and an expert archer. I am OK with a sword or dagger, but the bow is my weapon of choice, especially if I need stealth to achieve my goals.

As I was finishing my training, a young elf I did not recognise asked me to go to Resa's tent and wait, apparently our leader needed my help.

I respected her leadership and made my way towards the biggest tent in our town.

Just after I arrived, Resa entered and, after greetings had been exchanged, Resa said, "I have something for you."

She then went to her closet, where she proceeded to take out a dusty, bronze staff that was embedded with a worn, red jewel. She explained that it had belonged to my father and could be used to contain many spells that could be channelled outwards when required. She handed it to me, and I carefully took it. After thanking her, I asked why I needed it. Resa went on to explain to me that outside the town darkness was spreading and tainting the land, and she asked me to check this out for her, as one of most trusted heroes and also a good friend. Without hesitation I agreed, as I had always respected and trusted her words without question; she was our leader after all.

Knowing I would be away a while, I headed to my lodgings, what we elves call home, to get supplies for my trip; these included some food, water, a dagger, my trusty bow and arrows, my contact stone and some spell books, I also took some Xens, the currency used throughout the Joining.

As the staff was dusty, I decided to wipe it down using a wet cloth. I experienced a mixture of emotion while holding the staff; proud to follow my great father's footsteps, but saddened as I remembered his passing. Now being all prepared, I left my tent and made my way back to Resa's. I kissed her on the cheek and thanked her for the chance, as I had been bored lately with my old routine.

I was so pleased to be making my own story and was determined to prove it to myself and others. I hoped my parents would be proud of my upcoming adventure.

I walked towards The Moonshine Inn, and I saw a large crowd of people gathered on the way. Curious as to what could be so interesting, I made my way through the crowd to the centre where, to my amazement, stood a beautiful elven dancer.

She had blazing red hair, deep blue eyes, and a fair complexion. She was wearing a brilliant short skirt and a glittering top in a spectrum of colours. The elven lady was slender, about five foot six, and looked to be about twenty years old. She seemed to hypnotise the crowd with her graceful movements, and once the dancer had finished, the crowd dispersed looking happy and smiling.

This was my chance to tell the lady how impressed I was with her dancing. As I got closer to her, she looked familiar to me, and then I realised I had been right, it turned out to be my friend Rista. Oh, how she had grown more beautiful over the years we had been apart.

But as I stood opposite her, I was concerned about how she would react, so I just smiled nervously. Rista saw me staring after a while and, to my surprise, she reached out to hug me tightly. She explained she would recognise my smile anywhere.

I decided to ask how long she was in town for and offered to buy her a drink, so while making our way to the tavern, we reminisced about our past and what she had been up to since leaving our town.

Upon entering the tavern, we got lost in the din of bellowing, drunken voices and stayed close together, in case we were separated due to the pushing and bumping of the many races that were drinking there.

Rista found a table, while I suggested my favourite drink, known as a Flaming Phoenix because of its dark, complex honey taste and red glow. I went to the bar and ordered the drinks. Once they had been created, I took them, then returned to my friend, and we chatted as loudly as we dare. Once Rista had heard all about my new adventure, much to my shock, she agreed to go along with me, explaining that she always loved to challenge herself.

As our conversation was ending, the tavern door opened with a loud crash, and all went silent. Rista and I, along with most other drinkers, looked towards the door where two silhouettes stood.

As the silhouettes moved further into the tavern, I realised the reason for the inn going silent, there in my tavern was the swordsman who had helped me with my duelling skills, Blade the Masterful.

He stood out amongst the whole crowd. Even though he was a human, unlike most I have seen, he had a look of someone well groomed. His short, dark brown hair was clean and tidy, his deep hazel eyes were full of life and they gave him a ruggedly handsome look. All the ladies were swooning and blowing kisses to him, much to the annoyance of their husbands, but he just smiled and waved to them.

Blade was wearing a short shirt and trousers, his muscled arms showed his proud tattoo of two crossed swords, the mark of a powerful warrior, and strapped to his back was his large, heavy sword that everyone knew was his weapon of choice, as hardly anyone could outdo him in swordsmanship.

The other person was also well known; it was Magna the Great, a good friend of our leader and another human. Unlike Blade, who was a legendary warrior, he was a powerful mage with brown eyes and grey hair. He wore a bright red cloak, which had a gold lining and mysterious runes all over it, while his weapon of choice was a silver staff. Some of the older generation of elves, mainly the spellcasters, bowed to the wizard.

I decided to approach Blade and offer to buy him a drink with the hope of discussing the chance of him joining us on our journey, as this Darc phenomenon was concerning me.

As I approached Blade, he initially looked curiously at me; I was just an unknown elf. Much to my delight Blade, now more informed, remembered me from my impressive sword skills and he agreed that he and his friend Magna would join us.

Once I had bought both of the legends a drink, I made my way towards our table again, as I had just remembered about Rista who was looking rather upset. I apologised to her and explained about Blade and Magna, then grabbed two more seats.

Rista tried not to blush, as the warrior sat next to her, she hid her face away. We decided to work together to plan our next move. We knew we would need to leave Drake's Cliff so, finishing our drinks and paying the bill, our group left ready for our adventure together.

We passed many houses and shops. Without warning, a *Violet Spinner* spell swept us off our feet and, as we all tumbled through the air, we felt completely paralysed and at the same time we were carried out of the town. Sometime later, we were dumped onto the ground, very sore and bruised, and the spinner then dissolved.

After we got ourselves together, we couldn't really move and found ourselves in front of the main gate of Drake's Cliff, which had now been locked, while I spotted an eerie symbol revealing itself over the gate. We were all worried about the city, but we hoped that someone in one of the surrounding towns might know what the symbol meant or how it was going to affect the town.

All attempts, including magical ones, had no effect on the symbol, it just glowed an evil red colour. Any spell against it was nullified and weapon blows bounced off; whatever Darc magic had been used it was very powerful. We hoped everyone would be safe, as now no one could enter or leave.

My party decided to follow the usual path away from the town, as we began our long journey. We soon arrived at a large stone bridge which led over a flaming chasm.

As our group crossed the massive bridge, the flames appeared higher and more powerful; they moved as if controlled by a greater source. Yellows, reds and then vibrant oranges swirled around us, the heat was unbearable, and so we decided to make a run for it.

As we did, to our horror, the fire began taking shape, and large creatures appeared from it. To our utter amazement, we had encountered one of Rith's rarest monsters, ember beings. These large creatures were magma magic given life, they were vicious and strong and would use powerful blasts to roast anything in their way.

We fought back as best we could, Magna casting a few small aqua spells, but we all ended up with minor burns until I had an idea. I then pointed my staff straight up and cast the *Storm* spell, hoping it would work, as I had only tried it once before and ended up soaking me and my classmates.

Everyone else watched as the spell began. It turned the sky black and then the wind picked up, thunder filled the air, torrents of rain began to fall, while lightning split the sky above us. I was so proud; it was a powerful sight.

My three comrades found cover from the downpour under a rock formation. I was soaked, but grateful the spell worked. As the torrent of rain touched the beasts, they began to turn to mist and as soon as the wind caught them, they flew away.

With our path now clear and my storm beginning to ebb, we all made sure to heal our burns, and I used a lite breeze spell to dry myself off and we carried on our journey.

In a far-off place, blood-red eyes spied on our progress; someone was now furious!

My party and I safely crossed the bridge. Rista then explained that it led to a place called **The Scragged Copse** where she had done most of her dance training, but said she was surprised that we had encountered anything at all, as the bridge was usually clear with no flames.

We all followed Rista who led us through the Copse. Our path was filled with many beautiful plants of different shapes and colours, and it felt as if someone had grown a rainbow around us.

It was then I noticed one of the trees. It stood out because of its vivid green foliage and it had a weathered sign on it which read:

T easure i th s spo b foun when little cr atures fl around.

Confused, we all took turns reading the sign and eventually, as a group, realised that before it had weathered, it had read:

Treasure in this spot be found when little creatures fl y around.

As we all said this spell together aloud, a shower of sparkles in an array of colours filled the air. I heard many whispering voices, and we were soon surrounded by beautiful breeze sprites. One really stood out. It was slightly larger than the others and was an azure blue colour with shimmering, gold-flecked wings.

To my surprise it ignored me completely, instead flying around Rista. It then dropped a gold locket in her hand, after which it smiled and then it and its brethren vanished. So not to lose this precious gift, I popped it into my bag.

Once our path was clear, we followed it to a crossroads and decided to split up for a while to cover more land. Rista and I went into **Th e Mountain Pass**, while Magna and Blade headed to **Graven Vale Hollow**. We will catch up with them later.

Brightleaf Day 2

Rista and I traversed over many rocky paths, jagged mountains overshadowed us, and howls of unknown creatures could be heard in the distance. Everyone in Rith knew of powerful creatures that made the mountains their home. Rista was now showing off her agility to me by leaping and flipping over rocks, but unfortunately, she missed her timing and fell over a stone causing a mini rockslide. I checked she was OK but then the entire ground shook.

We looked up and got the shock of lives. Looming above us was a great Chillern dragon wearing a silver collar. It began spewing ice blasts out of its mouth while slowly descending, making ready to attack.

I thought very quickly and pointed my staff towards the dragon, casting *Rainbow Ricochet*. As the spell hit, a huge net in an array of colours was formed, plunging the beast to the ground and leaving it trapped and dazed. Once I was sure the dragon wasn't going anywhere, I made my way towards the creature and noticed its eyes were covered in a Darc cloud. I realised, to my utter disgust, that this majestic dragon must have been controlled and assumed that was the reason for the collar and its aggression towards us.

A voice, which seemed to come from nowhere, agreed and it said, "That's the second one I've seen."

Startled, I turned around to be confronted by a cloaked figure, who stood ready to attack. Rista and I watched as, out of thin air, she conjured an ornate, white staff. Ready to protect ourselves from the deadly stranger, we both prepared for battle.

Rista was determined to defend herself and so she lunged at the stranger with her dagger, but the newcomer countered using an *Aqua Blast*. This spell blew Rista away and, soaked and dazed, I saw her fall to the ground. After immobilising Rista, I saw that the figure had now thrown off her cloak.

Underneath her disguise stood the most beautiful stranger I had ever seen. She looked slightly older than me, and her brown hair, green eyes, and fair complexion added to her beauty. With the cloak now on the ground, my gaze took in what she was wearing. The short top and skirt were breathtaking, hugging every curve of her body, but I knew she was also deadly, the fact she conjured a staff out of nowhere warned me of that.

Knowing I needed to defend myself, I prepared my own spell, one I knew very well. I chose to cast *Rainbow Ricochet* again, but the woman countered it and hit back with a *Golden Grip* spell. I had no time to disarm the spell and found my body was bound by a set of golden ropes and I was unable to attack. Both my arms and legs were pinned to my sides, and my staff lay next to me but I had no way of getting to it.

Stuck fast, all I could do was watch her come towards me. I feared the worst, but to my surprise, instead of hurting me, she seemed to be looking at my face. I could see her staring intently into my blue eyes; it was quite nerve-wracking. I heard her whisper something, and all I remember is hearing her voice before I drifted off into a deep sleep.

When I awoke, I felt different and, to my shock, I was now upright and holding my staff. The lady stood in front of me and smiled. I was perplexed, as the last thing I remember was lying pinned to the ground.

Once I had got my bearings, I began firing questions at her, but she just smiled.

When I finally stopped my barrage of questions, she began to speak and said, "I'm sorry about pinning you down, but when I saw you trying to hurt that poor creature, I had to help defend it. You see, my name is Serenity. I am known throughout Rith as the Protector of Dragons."

After the apology, I explained to her why I had stunned the dragon and was not trying to hurt it, having learnt many years ago that most dragons were not dangerous unless provoked. This seemed to help and I followed by introducing myself to her. We chatted for a few minutes more, then I saw Rista now getting to her feet. She was still soaked and angry that she had been attacked, and she ignored Serenity completely, but she made sure I was OK.

Deciding not to be rude, and much to Rista's reluctance, I chose to introduce her to Serenity. I could see the ladies exchange evil looks and, deciding not to interfere, I changed my view about trying to get these two to get along and instead I said our goodbyes and led a seething Rista away.

Hi all, I am Serenity, pleased to meet you. So, after my first encounter with your heroes, let me continue the story.

I walked towards the powerful beast and made sure to stay far enough away but near enough so that I could disarm Tarum's spell. The dragon was now free but still dazed and immobile, and I walked confidently towards it.

When I was closer, I found it was wearing a silver collar tight to its neck. The collar was filled with deep black gemstones that buzzed with power. I had to get this thing off it, so I pointed my staff at it and powered up a blast of pure magma magic. As the blast hit the collar, it began to melt and slid off the dragon's throat; luckily the dragon was unharmed.

I knew the dragon was grateful that I'd helped it. Slowly, it managed to open its huge wings and flew high into the blue sky.

Knowing how loyal dragons were and that my kindness would be repaid, I decided to name the dragon Chill.

Once the dragon was free, I saw that Tarum and Rista had not got too far. I called to them, hoping that I hadn't been too hasty and missed my chance for some more help with my mission. Luckily, Tarum headed back towards me followed by Rista.

I knew Rista would be wary of my motives after my attack; I didn't blame her, but I was only doing my duty.

It was nice to meet you all, I'm sure I will be back. Let's hand back to Tarum, he is getting impatient, I can see his foot tapping.

I was pleased when Serenity called out, as I knew I needed more help than just three people. The is dark magic was really worrying me, and it had been on my mind ever since our joyride out of my home town and the eerie symbol appearing on its gate.

So, when we were back with Serenity, she thanked us for returning and then proceeded to tell us her trouble and why she was out adventuring. It turned out that she was trying to free the dragons from the grip of a Darc villain called Mysi, Lord of the Undead, and that he was looking for the Sphere of Time, a unique, crafted artefact of great power that, in the wrong hands, could cause utter chaos.

As she recalled this artefact, something sparked in my memory and I remembered Resa telling me a story about the sphere many years ago. As I thought she would, Serenity also knew the story and began telling us both about it.

"According to the story, The Magnificent himself had made a sphere out of all the elements so it could help control time and the seasons. But on using it and seeing its power first-hand, he was worried that if it fell into evil hands the power would rip Xexus apart, as everyone would fight to control it. So instead of using it, he sealed it within a mountain in the highest part of Rith known as **The Great Spire**."

When she had finished telling us the tale, Rista and I were both amazed and curious but eager to find this mysterious artefact just to see if it really was as powerful as legend said.

Serenity went on to explain that an ancient library on the continent of **Mudrift** might have evidence of its existence. It was a note from an old explorer known as Prof. Huntsmen. He had discovered an ancient runic scroll which, when deciphered, read: *"My sphere will stay for none to see till a circle of scales uncovers me."*

I had now realised that it was Mysi who had cursed my town, and I vowed to stop him and free my people. Serenity asked if she could join us. I saw Rista grimace at the thought, but as leader of this group it was my choice, so Serenity joined us, as our duo became a trio.

Up above us, we all saw the clouds form evil words; they read: *"I WILL HAVE MY WAY, YOU WILL ALL PERISH."*

I knew we had to find the source of the evil, as now someone was out to get me not just my city. Who and why I had no clue, but I surmised that a bigger and more powerful villain was running the show, so we had to move fast. After another long and tiring trek, we finally reached the exit of the pass.

Glad to leave the danger-filled area, we made our way to the only town in this mountainous region that I knew, it was called **Lithania**.

It was very late when we arrived, and the town looked a lot like my own town Drake's Cliff, it was also surrounded by a huge stone wall, and the only entrance was a big wooden gate. I tried to enter, but it was locked tight.

So, our trio decided to sit outside the gate on a group of flat rocks. I took my food and water from my bag and we all shared a well-earned rest together. Sometime later and now feeling better, we all heard a bolt go back and found that the locked gate was being opened.

Serenity, Rista, and I walked through the gate into the town, but we were now concerned for our safety, as we were puzzled about how the gate had opened. On closer examination, we saw no one at the gatehouse.

We walked through the silent town, until I found an alley where there was a dim light. Intrigued, I told the others who followed me towards it. On following the light, we arrived outside a large store, where a sign swinging above us read: "***Lightning's Guild***, *all adventurers welcome.*"

Rista pushed in front of me, intrigued by the shop. She tried the door and, sure enough, it opened. We all stepped through and walked past many shelves full of powerful weapons, shining armour, and found an extensive collection of coloured scrolls. Most were locked away in wooden cabinets with see-through glass panels.

We made our way towards the counter on the far side of the shop. At the counter a human female with bright yellow eyes stood, she had jet-black hair filled with silver streaks.

She looked happy to see us and asked, "What can I do for you?"

My party explained about our long journey and that we were looking for supplies.

Serenity asked the lady if she had any potions. The shop assistant then produced a list that told us the prices in Xens. Serenity bought three Life Potions and a Potion of Firestart.

The lady behind the counter was intrigued at her purchase and said that, "Those items are generally bought by people who expect to run into trouble."

Meanwhile, Rista and I were chatting about our encounter with Serenity and the spell Mysi had cast, and I didn't notice that the lady was now eavesdropping.

Hi, adventurers. Remember my introduction at the beginning of the book? I will now leave Tarum and tell my short story to move this adventure along. I hope you are all ready, as I'm about to start.

When I heard this story, my yellow eyes lit up. I smiled to myself and walked casually out from behind the counter, then began looking busy, pretending to stack the shelves, all the while preparing a way to stop the trio leaving.

I needed all of them, so I slipped past them towards the entrance and stood in front of the door barring their exit, which put them on high alert; they were prepared to defend themselves. Impressed by the three adventurers, I chose to let my guard down, back away, and began explaining about why I didn't want them to leave.

Thankfully, they gave me the benefit of the doubt and listened to my story, but they kept their weapons ready just in case. I introduced myself as Lightning and went on to explain that I owned the shop. I had heard the name Mysi before in connection with an evil, dragon-like lord known as Blood Bone, and it was him who was giving the orders to Mysi. I also told them about a captured black dragon and a human healer who were held captive in a sinister place, while Mysi was now going after the rest of the dragons.

I thanked them for listening to my story and said I would let them go on the condition that they were too free both captives and help free any other dragons that they came across. They all agreed.

So now you know more about me, but not everything, and with that revelation, I will take my leave. Let's check back in with Tarum. With a new challenge ahead of us, we continued our journey, and we all left the shop. To our surprise, we had been so intrigued by Lightning's story that when we left the shop it was now morning.

The whole town was alive, people were chatting noisily as their kids ran through the streets, many people were opening their stores and the local tavern, known as **The Travellers Arms**, was now accepting patrons, while the rats waited under the stalls ready to pounce on the many delights that the people had to offer.

Serenity and I were chatting about Lightning and her quest. We asked around the town, but no one had heard of Lightning's Guild or Lightning. We were all puzzled, as we knew that we had not imagined the shop or the new information about this evil, as Serenity was still carrying the potions.

Once out of the town, we followed another path and came to a raging river. The only way to cross it was a tattered looking wooden bridge. We all gritted our teeth and headed towards it.

Rista and I went first. As we stepped on the bridge, it swayed beneath our feet. We then heard worrying sounds of cracking, as many of the splintered planks that we had already used fell into the water below us. Just as we thought we were safe, we heard an enormous splash and now underneath our feet, in the water below us, swam a huge Finnark. This shark like creature swam back and forth waiting for one of us to topple off the bridge and into its hungry jaws.

Serenity was lucky and had followed us before the planks had fallen. All around us the planks still fell, cutting off any chance of going forwards or back, leaving us all stranded in the centre of the bridge on a weakening plank.

Worried, I realised that my only hope to change our fate was to try the spell called *Last Resort*. Even though I had never been allowed to use it, as it was strong magic, Resa had secretly taught me the spell.

I raised my staff and drew a unique shape in the air, and a green spark appeared. At first nothing happened. Then, just as the last plank had slipped into the water and our group were about to plunge into the raging river and hungry jaws, the spark became a green glow, encasing us all, and then our party was gone.

When I reappeared, I was in total darkness. I called out each person's name to check everyone was ok. As I was awaiting a response, I saw something within the darkness. Just then, a large glow filled the whole cave with a powerful, bright light. As I knew the only other person with magic in our trio was Serenity, I reminded myself to thank her.

As the spell took hold, the whole place was illuminated. It showed us the cave's structure and its underground beauty.

The cave was composed of stalactites and stalagmites that were forming all around us. We saw shallow pools of clear water and different fungi and mushrooms growing on the damp walls. Now able to see the well-trodden path ahead of us, we all began to follow it deeper into the cave. After an hour or so later, we found the exit but wished that we had not.

The ladies and I stepped out of the cave and onto a wet patch of earth. On reading the roughly painted sign, we had come out on **Black Wood Bog**.

This was a place that once discovered would never be forgotten, as the stories of the many people who lost their lives there were still told to this day. As these were horrific tales of missing people and even talk of murder, we decided to stick together and tread carefully while avoiding obstacles like fallen branches, tree stumps, and the like. We all made our way through the large swamp, and after many hours of wandering, filthy, hungry, and tired, our group found a little island and decided to rest.

Brightleaf Day 3

As night drew in, I noticed the swamp change. Large bats flew overhead while hunting for prey, and snakes and other creatures could be heard slithering through the pools and reeds.

We were all fascinated with the sounds of Black Wood Bog and listened intently. Soon, we all heard an unusual noise. It sounded like claws scratching the ground and then, with no warning, an eerie mist surrounded us. We could not see anything at first. As my group became accustomed to it, I saw flashes of silver. Scared, I tried not to panic, but when we heard the sound of dragging footsteps that panic intensified.

I had no idea what the footsteps belonged to and dreaded finding out.

My fears were right for, as the fog lifted, the real horror of the steps was revealed. There before us stood some midnight bones. These skeletal creatures were earlier casualties of the bog, that had risen from their swampy grave to seek out the living for food, and they carried long, rusted weapons stained with the blood of long dead victims.

Still tired and filthy, my friends and I avoided the skeletons as best we could, but soon the midnight bones had us surrounded and then a few of the group of evil creatures began to head towards us. Just as all seemed lost, something extraordinary happened to me.

It was like I had a new energy coursing through my entire body, and I felt more invigorated and powerful than ever before. The other strange thing was that my surroundings had changed and my friends and the midnight bones were completely still. A large, white glow was now emanating from me. As I moved my body, the light followed; it was like a second skin.

I decided to try something, so I made a swirling motion with my hands. As I was beginning to expect, the light followed. I kept practising and had soon mastered my new technique. Hoping that my new skill would come in handy, I waved my hands towards one skeleton. A blast of pure lite magic flew towards my target and, sure enough, as it hit the target, it exploded sending shards of bones everywhere.

Finally able to turn the tide of the battle, I used my new skill to destroy the remaining skeletons. As the last one fell, everything went black.

When I awoke, I saw my two comrades standing over me, concern etched on their faces. I was eager to share my new skill with them, but realised that the second skin I had earlier was gone, and as I ran through my knowledge of lite spells, I couldn't remember the lite blast. I was very puzzled, as I remembered Resa telling me the only way you could use a spell was if you had learned it, and she had never taught me that one. Trying not to think too much about it, we continued our journey.

Realising that the island was not safe, and not wanting

to encounter anything else, we found shelter in the hollow of a massive tree and decided to use it to rest and recuperate. It would work well, as it was both warm, dry, and had only one entrance so there was little chance of an ambush.

My friends and I decided to finish off my food and water, we then all laid down to rest. Once morning had come, we all awoke to find someone had been there sometime in the night. Both Rista and I each found a bag with our names embossed on them on the floor of the tree.

Eager to see what we had been given, but also wary, we both opened our bags. I was over the moon, as mine contained an Oakwood Bow and Slender-Wood Arrows. I knew that the arrows were the best of their kind and were unlikely to miss their target, as I had practised with one of them at Resa's Lea, but had never owned any, or the bow to use them with, because they cost a small fortune and with my small wage it would have taken me years to buy a set.

Once my bag had been opened, it was Rista's turn. Seeing my new bow and arrows, she opened her bag, tipped it out, but found nothing of interest just a plain tree branch.

Puzzled, I saw her keep looking at it and then watched as a strange expression appeared on her face, as if it was joke. Just as she was about to lose her temper and throw the branch away, my open bag began glowing. I told her to reach inside it as, having been around unusual experiences throughout my life, I knew that the glowing must have been connected to the plain branch.

To all of our surprise, she pulled her hand out and held between her fingers was the chain of a locket. Looking more closely, I saw that the locket was made of a gleaming silver; a very rare mineral found throughout Xexus. The locket itself was shaped like a large tree. I saw her run her hand around the side of the jewellery, she undid the catch, and suddenly a kaleidoscope of colour escaped from it and began to wind itself around the branch.

We then heard small giggles. As each colour faded, more of the branch was revealed. It had turned from something plain to something utterly amazing, as the sprites magic had manipulated the branch into a slim, golden sword with a large handle shaped like a sprite's head.

As she admired the sword, we heard a strange noise. We looked at the locket, and it began to rust and tarnish. Her beautiful keepsake had gone and in its place was a miserable looking object. Still all confused and surprised by the locket and branch, we headed back on our adventure and, after a long walk, found ourselves at the bottom of a large hill. We stowed the broken locket back in my bag, not wanting to leave it behind.

Glad to be further away from the bog, we climbed to the top of the hill via a little path. A magnificent temple was nestled amongst some trees, and of course, being an inquisitive bunch, we decided to explore it.

Upon entering the temple, we found it to be spectacular; stained-glass windows shimmered in the sunlight, and marble pillars and statues stood proudly.

On closer examination, we saw that something looked out of place. There, in the centre of the room, we found the whole roof of the temple was missing, all that was left were some stone chunks that littered the floor

I saw that the wooden altar had been knocked over and the candles that once surrounded it lay discarded. We knew some sort of battle must have been fought there.

I found Serenity looking at something, and following her gaze, I saw that she was checking out the floor around the altar.

Between us, we picked up some things shimmering on the floor; iridescent scales were strewn all over it. They were beautiful, formed of different shades of red. I saw Serenity begin to sob. Between sobs, she told me they were tail scales from a scarlet dragon and, to our horror, we realised that Mysi must have captured another dragon, as Lightning had previously suggested.

Upset and angry, we left the damaged temple through the far exit. We knew where to go, as the poor creature's scales littered the path ahead of us.

After exiting the temple, we all arrived on a grassy bank. As we were just about to step on it, we felt the whole ground beneath us shake violently. Slowly, we felt ourselves lift off the ground; a rather unpleasant experience and one I don't want to repeat too often.

Unable to stay grounded, we toppled off and fell. Both Serenity and I fell face first but Rista landed gracefully and helped us to our feet. Once we had got ourselves together, we prepared to battle the now mound of earth which, in fact, had been a dormant type of elemental known as a terrain beast. It had been dozing in the shade and was now angry at being disturbed. I cast a spell. I chose an *Aqua Blast* just as Serenity had been able to cast *Bitter Wind*. Unbeknown to us, as the two spells sped towards the creature, to our bewilderment and the fright of the scared beast, the two spells began to twist and merge to form a mirage.

As the image became more stable, another being was now floating in front of us. This beautiful, ethereal creature was completely transparent.

She spoke to us, and I could hear a bitter tone in her voice which said, "I am Crystalia one of the Icilia. We beings of magic are sometimes summoned to protect the innocent. This poor creature has done you no harm, leave it be, and if you do not, I will destroy you."

I saw that Serenity was looking confused having known nothing about this race of creatures. Neither did I, and we decided to heed her warning, so we all agreed to the Icilia's demand and the beast, now calm, fell back to sleep. With her work done and the spells gone, Crystalia began to fade but warned us her race were many, and if ever we killed an innocent, no matter how we did it, something bad would happen. After leaving her warning, she faded from our view and we carried on our adventure.

This adventure so far was unexpected, but I felt alive and eager to explore more of my realm.

All three of us were determined to live by Crystalia guidance but knew that we still needed to find and free this missing dragon. We surged forwards with our quest and came to one of my favourite places in Rith, known locally as **Beast Falls**.

The reason behind this was the uniquely shaped waterfall that could be found there. Its crystal-clear water flowed over three levels of rocks, ending in a deep pool filled with all sorts of aquatic creatures. On the ground around it were huge statues rumoured, amongst the local people, to have been placed by The Magnificent himself.

We wanted to rest, so I took my water bottle out of my bag and began filling it from the pool. I saw Rista practising her moves and, after filling my bottle, I found a nice spot under a pair of unicorn statues that also provided some much-needed shade.

I took out my spell books. As this adventure was becoming much more interesting, I wanted to have a few more spells up my sleeve in case we encountered any more unwelcome beasts.

As I was settling down, I saw Serenity walking away, but decided to leave her as, even though we travelled together, I did not really know her that well and guessed she had her own ideas.

Hi all, Serenity here. So, you have followed Tarum's path so far, but I bet you want to know why I left the other two and what happened. Well, you're in luck, as I have decided to tell you.

First, a little about me. I was born and raised on the third continent in the Joining, Volcania. From a young age, my parents noticed my affinity with magic that in time, and with practice, could be used to help dragons. They decided to teach me more about it, my mum being a powerful mage and my dad a professor. He went missing a few years ago, that's what spurred me to leave Volcania and try and find him, but anyway, back to the story.

I walked away from Tarum and Rista. In truth I was upset, not only had I not been left a gift, but my heart was breaking thinking about that poor dragon and its missing scales.

I walked teary-eyed along a dirt path and passed a large statue that caught my eye. I wiped my eyes and took a closer look and, sure enough, it was of someone I recognised. I was very suspicious; why would there be a statue of a shopkeeper at Beast Falls?

I was still puzzling this, when something unexpected happened. To my surprise, the statue began to glow. I rubbed my eyes, but the glow was still there. Then I felt the magic plane tingle, something I had learned before I left my home, and I knew something powerful was stirring. Concerned for my safety, I moved away from the statue and hid behind a large tree.

It was lucky I had because, as I peeked out from behind the tree, I saw the glow get brighter. Soon, a white light had obscured my vision. I then felt light-headed and collapsed to the ground. When I came to, I looked upwards and froze; someone was looming over me, someone powerful and utterly amazing.

I stayed silent for a while, taking in my situation, then she spoke, and my silence was broken.

She said, "My dearest, Serenity, it is I, Lightning. As you can clearly see, I am more than just a mere shopkeeper. I am, in fact, the high guardian of Rith, and my elemental powers are connected to lite magic. I brought you and Tarum together, as you will be a great asset to him. Thank for your loyal service and, in case you wondered, I did get you a gift, but it was too important to leave."

Her actual guardian form was empowering to me. She was wearing a white and blue, crystal-covered dress that tapered at the waist, showing every feminine curve of her body. Her black hair now had more silver and white strands and was long, wavy, and luxurious. She wore a silver and blue cape across her shoulders that flowed like water behind her, and her staff of choice was a white wood staff that was topped by a silver, round sphere.

I was so enchanted by her true form; I didn't see her point the staff at me. The only time I noticed anything different was when I felt a hot liquid run through my body, it was like my blood was on fire. I fell to the ground in agony, worry filling my mind. Had I been tricked? Was this just all a ruse?

To my surprise, as suddenly as the pain came, it started to subside. My mind started to relax, my worry dissipated and then I felt it, a new power hidden within me. I now knew more magma spells then before. I could summon Magma Blasts, Fire

Twisters, and even create a Fire Mannequin. These spells were so powerful, I was nervous about even trying them.

As I became more confident, I looked back at Lightning. The guardian had a friendly smile waiting and two lots of equipment in her open hands.

The first was the most enchanting and beautiful hooded cloak I had ever seen. As she handed it to me, I was in awe. I ran the material through my fingers and, to my surprise, it felt hot to the touch. When I had got used to the heat, I took a closer look and saw it was embroidered with a large magma symbol as its centrepiece and the rest of the pattern was an intricate gold design.

I asked Lightning about it, and she went on to explain that another guardian had hand created it, and with it, all my magma magic would be stronger. She added that it was known as the Cloak of Red Fire.

The second item was a large, hand-carved, wooden staff. Runes ran the length of its handle, and it was topped with a dark red ruby. As I held it in my hand, it thrummed with power. She told me it was known as a Magma Rod. I was so engrossed by the two items that when Lightning spoke again my attention was split, but knowing her new position, I knew I had to listen.

She went on to explain that Blood Bone was actually her brother, something that made me curse under my breath, and that was how she knew of his plans to capture the dragons. He was using his most powerful adviser to help him, Mysi, known locally the Lord of the Undead. Mysi wanted to control the sphere to command the power of her realm and so the two devious villains' influence was spreading through her continent, that's why she needed help to stop them.

She also said that she wanted the others to learn of her true identity in their own time. She began to end the conversation by explaining that I was now an Ember Mistress and could manipulate the power of magma magic to my will. She offered to look after the cloak and staff until I needed them, as my journey might differ to the others'. Puzzled, we concluded our conversation and she vanished.

As I wandered back, I found her statue again. To my utter amazement, at the foot of the statue was an unusual piece of jewellery. When I picked it up, I saw it was an amulet. Hanging on the bottom of the silver chain was a large, black dragon with open wings.

Next to it was a small piece of paper with just the letter L on. I knew it was a gift from Lightning and wore it with pride.

When I finally arrived back to my friends, they began questioning me, but all I said was that I went for a walk and lost track of time. Tat seemed to convince them and, between us, we managed to locate a well-hidden path and followed it to a town. Th e small sign read "*Welcome to* **Middleton**".

Thank you for your time and energy listening to my part of the story. Now back to our hero Tarum, as he continues leading you through his adventure.

We all walked through the open wooden gate that must have been unlocked earlier, as this dwarven town was known to be popular with merchants. We began exploring the town, walking further up a stone slab road. I spied a little corner stall that sold some sort of hot meat. Thinking it would be ideal to take some with me, I made my way to it. But no sooner had I grabbed it and placed it in my bag, we heard a horn being blown. Guessing this was not a good sign, we prepared to defend ourselves as we had no idea what the horn signified.

Once the horn had stopped, the whole of the town seemed busier but, as we would discover, this town was not what it seemed, as every new resident that appeared looked angry. Every man, woman, and some children had a purple tinge to the skin and blood-red eyes.

They held a variety of objects that included frying pans, swords and even a broom. A broad male, leading the charge, carried a darc banner with the same symbol that had appeared on my town's gate. I knew then Mysi must have put a spell on them and turned them into his Darc puppets. Now I was torn; I didn't want to hurt these people, but they were definitely not going to let us pass.

So, after putting a plan into place, we battled the townsfolk using mainly defence spells and caused only light wounds to them. Luckily, as the townsfolk weren't that skilled, we managed to lock them back into their houses and hoped that if we could defeat Mysi their minds would be turned back to normal

The battle had taken it out of all of us, and both Serenity and I were low on magic. Deciding that this town was too dangerous to stay in, we made our way to the exit, but as we arrived at the gate, another larger dwarf stood in our way.

We had to leave the town so knew we needed to beat this last dwarf as he was guarding the only exit. As we drew nearer to him, I saw a puzzled look cover Rista's face. Knowing to trust her judgment, I prepared a small offensive spell just in case I needed to fight. To our surprise, unlike the townsfolk, this dwarf held out his hand. We saw he had normal eyes, so made our decision to give him the benefit of the doubt, hoping we hadn't walked into a trap.

He walked towards me and shook my hand, then introduced himself as Rugland. I checked him out; he certainly wasn't like any dwarf I had encountered. He had wild, black hair and carried a bag with an assortment of weapons. I saw another pouch that I assumed was probably full of Xens.
I made this assumption because, as he moved, I heard them chinking together. He went on to tell us he was a mercenary for hire and had crossed paths with Mysi on many occasions.

From his recent jobs and clients, he had learnt that Mysi's grip was strongest on four towns within Rith, these were **Riddleton, Shadowsville, Trollstone,** and **Purestrom.**

I got the impression that he was hiding something, as whenever he mentioned Mysi, Rugland's tone changed to a bitter one.

With this new information in hand, we went to leave the town, but Rugland told us that the path beyond the exit was impassable due to a large cluster of mountains. He explained that the only way out of the town, apart from the way that we'd come, was to enter **The Under-Caves** that had been carved by his race's ancestors, and he warned us to be careful as it could be quite challenging. After taking us to the entrance of the caves, he left. I hoped to see him again, as I was determined and would do whatever it took to learn of his connection to the mage who'd cursed my town.

We made our way down the sloping tunnel that led to the entrance. Rista found some more dragon scales and followed them. After a while, we all arrived at the beginning of a dark mass of caves and tunnels.

Not sure which one to follow, we all chose the biggest, as this had another pile of scales. Unfortunately, something nasty lived in this tunnel and even now was stalking us. Once the ladies and I had reached a certain point in the tunnel, something pounced and, before we could attack, we were all pinned to the tunnel wall by a rancid-smelling, brown web.
We then found out what had ambushed us and full-on terror ran through us all.

In front of us was one of the deadliest beasts that could be found across our world, a gigantic arachnid that we knew as an Arania. It had a large, furry body, eight eyes, long, hairy legs, and a set of fangs that were like switchblades. As it was about to feast on us, we saw drops of purple venom coating its mouth. We were nearly out of options, as we were all stuck fast.

Hi all, sorry to interrupt. It's me, Serenity. I would like to tell you how I saved our lives; no thanks needed, just throw xens.

So, as Tarum said, we were all stuck fast. Luckily, my new spells could be cast without a staff by using just my mind, so I cast *Fiery Force*. I focused on the web and soon it began to smoke. Seeing the smoke, the huge Arania became wary and it backed away. What the beast did not realise was the smoke was just a distraction.

Because behind the smoke a searing heat flicked across each strand of web that held us fast. Soon it had completely disintegrated and then, with nothing to hold us, we all fell to the ground. My fellow adventurers had minor burns but, other than that, were unharmed.

Now we had a new problem, as we still had to deal with the deadly Arania that was making its way back to us. Now free, I saw Rista run towards the beast. Thinking she was crazy, I watched as she plunged the sprite's head sword into one of its legs, just as it took a swipe at her with its scorpion tail, its sharp point just missing her arm. I was utterly shocked as, in all my years of journeying through Xexus, I had never seen an Arania with this appendage. It was then I knew Mysi had created this creature; it was not a normal Arania.

I saw the Arania's leg buckle, and it wobbled. Seeing this advantage, I watched Tarum cast his own spell which impressed me, as he managed to cast a high-level spell with ease.

I watched on as the *Adaption* spell took hold. The ground below the beast began to move, and slowly it started to change and sink in on itself; the earth and mud becoming a large, churning eddy. The Arania began to sink, its large build slowly slipping further into the depths. I then looked at Rista and saw her look deflated, because as the evil creature sunk completely it took her beautiful sword with it, as Tarum had not realised that the sword was still attached to the beast.

With the threat taken care of, we regrouped, healed our wounds, and carried on further into The Under-Caves which had got much wider. As we pressed on, then entered another chamber, I saw a bleeding scarlet dragon chained to the cave wall.

Ignoring the warning looks from my two friends, I walked towards the great beast and got the dragon's attention by whistling. Unusually, the whistle, instead of being taken as friendly, enraged it, and it began to struggle against its chains. I saw the walls holding the chains start to crack. As I suspected, without the Arania guarding it, this beast was very angry.

Tarum and Rista started to run backwards to safety. I wasn't afraid, I stood in front of my friends, while trying to tap into all my inner strength and understanding of these great beasts. I then remembered something I had learnt in my early days as a dragon protector. Using my staff, I banged the ground twice, while a purple aura began to surround me, as the others looked on both shocked and amazed.

I began to sing softly and hypnotically to the dragon and, as I did this, the dragon's rage subsided.

When I finished my song the glow around me faded, but the dragon was now looking at me entranced by my power. He bowed to me, and I knew then I now had its respect. I named him Pyre. Free from his chains, the dragon tested his wings and, once he was satisfied, they were OK, he gave me once last glance, nodded his head, and shot straight up. That would have been great, had we not been underground, because as he crashed through the cave's ceiling it began to cave in.

Thank you for listening. I hope you liked seeing my skills with dragons. Now I will hand back to Tarum.

Thanks, Serenity. Now, as you already know, the caves were crumbling around us. Rista, Serenity, and I dashed our way through and, after hours of misleading tunnels and dead ends, we emerged at last from Th e Under-Caves, tired and wounded, into the town of Shadowsville.

We were all cautious on entering this town, as we had learned earlier it was currently in the grip of Mysi, but we were looking for rest and recuperation so had no choice.

We walked towards the entrance of Shadowsville and were confronted by two burly guards who asked, in a gruff manner, "Who are you? State your business."

I explained our predicament and requested to speak to someone in power. One guard let us all through, as the other headed away to get their leader. Once inside the town, we were greeted by Mikia the leader of Shadowsville. He was a short, plump man covered in a thick robe, and he wore a heavy, gold medallion that seemed to make him even shorter, though we all tried not to laugh at this.

Mikia said normally there would be no problem to let us stay, but a terrible curse was threatening the town. It appeared Mysi had transformed the souls of most of the townsfolk into his own army of spirit slaves and could control the minds and bodies of his victims.

Mikia noticed our group were ready for adventure and asked us to help find a way to break the spell on the town. He hinted that maybe a lady called Helen Zek could help. Promising to help, but unable to at the moment, we decided to head to the capital of Rith, **Mirrorwood**, as this was where Rista and I were to meet Blade and Magna anyway.

Serenity told us that it was quicker by air. I was confused, how could we travel by air? But she just smiled cheekily, then led us to a clear spot on a large mound on the outskirts of town.

She opened her bag and took out one large jewel which was ice blue in colour. Both Rista and I had no idea that Serenity carried gems in her bag, and she placed it on the ground and asked us to step back.

She then began chanting an incantation. We saw the gem begin to glow. A large, blue, shimmering shadow appeared and started to turn into a great shape. As we watched awestruck, it grew more robust. Its wings formed, then its long tail, and soon a giant dragon had arisen from the gem. It nuzzled its new mistress; she smiled proudly and then Chill lay flat on the ground.

Serenity showed us how to board him without causing him harm. Reluctantly, both Rista and I followed her example. After a quick lesson in steering, we took to the skies with the currents to help us. We both realised that Serenity must have had past experience riding dragons. We were both impressed by her skill, but nervous to be in the air; elves didn't really fly, they preferred being on the ground.

We began out on our long journey. The trip took about half a day or so, without any issues, and we soon arrived, about mid-evening, in Mirrorwood.

Serenity located a decent place to land, and slowly the dragon made its way down to the ground. It felt weird to feel the dragon's body slow down after riding it quite fast. Once on the ground and off our mount, I saw Serenity use a spell I was familiar with; she cast *Transform*. This spell always impresses me, as it can turn something solid into something else. I watched as our mighty beast began to fade and its body turned into a twisting smoke that headed back towards the gem.

I saw Serenity pick up the jewel and place it back into her bag. Rista seemed completely enthralled by the spell, but I managed to get her back to reality. As we were all visiting and meeting here, everyone knew that this temple was the main monument of Mirrorwood and we needed to see it, so we made our way to the massive structure that was known throughout Xexus as **The Temple of Rith**.

Our trio made our way inside. The beauty and craftsmanship of the place made me smile. Huge, imposing pillars carved with intricate symbols stood proudly. Dotted across the vast hall were long, silver banners with ornate, gold letter Rs that were entwined with unique, star-shaped Markus flowers. These were the symbol of our continent, and were named after a great artist who inspired the construction of the temple itself but who had died just after it has been finished, these floras came in a hue of vibrant colours. The ones of the banner were Red, Purple and White. We passed into the central room and walked past the rows of red, velvet cushions that lined the temple. Here people would pray and honour their guardian.

As we got to the very centre, an enormous, gold statue dominated the space. It was a version of The Magnificent with his hand holding the Sphere of Time. Th e aura of power it sent out ran through my entire body, and I knew whoever had sculpted it was a superior craftsman.

I was amazed, not only had Resa's story been correct, but I never thought I would get to see these sorts of things. I smiled to myself and realised I had come a long way since being a lowly mage from Drake's Cliff and was now more determined than ever to find the sphere and help all the cursed lands.

We all explored some more and located five smaller statues that had been placed, each one representing a different guardian. I knew this by reading the plaques next to each, and we found another one which was a lot bigger than the others and was of a young woman in a great pose, holding a giant spear pointing towards the sky. Her plaque read "*Lightning, High Guardian of Lite*".

Both Rista and I looked at each other shocked that our friend the shopkeeper was actually our land's guardian. To our surprise, Serenity seemed unfazed at this startling news, in fact she was smiling.

As we turned to leave, a bright beam of light blinded us. It filled the room and bounced off all the different objects, and the whole temple shimmered like a thousand diamonds. When the light had faded, there in the temple stood Lightning. She was about nine foot tall and glowing brightly. Both Rista and I were slightly scared to see her, but we had many questions. We saw that Lightning held in her hands a beautiful cape made to look like pure fire, swirls of colour dancing over it, and in her other hand a red staff glowed powerfully. Every now and then a red spark would follow a pattern from the top of the staff to the bottom.

Serenity walked towards her friend and bowed. Lightning then handed her the two magical items and explained to us that Serenity was now an ember mistress. This meant she was more powerful and had better control over magma spells, plus she could manage all types of dragons.

Rista and I were now even more confused, so Lightning explained, in greater detail, how she was the High Guardian of Lite and the daughter of The Magnificent and how she had been watching over us and helping when she could, as Rith was her domain. Then she told Serenity that to fnd the sphere and defeat Mysi we would need more help.

As I heard the truth, something clicked. I remembered the time earlier when I had defeated the midnight bones; it must have been with Lightning's help. That's when it happened, my confidence waned. I had always suffered with my own self-belief, it's one of the reasons I'd wanted to go on this adventure.

Lightning then led us all outside and to the edge of a massive cliff; it was very late now and the stars and moon were out.

As we needed more help, I explained to Serenity about Magna and Blade and knew, if she could find them, they would help. Lightning agreed with this and so, with a new task ahead of us, I saw Serenity head towards the cliff and begin chanting. At first nothing happened, then a huge shadow appeared over the moon and was heading towards us. Rista and I stood a little back not knowing what to expect.

To our surprise, a scarlet dragon appeared in front of the cliff. I saw Serenity nod to him and realised that it was Pyre, the dragon she had rescued from The Under-Caves.

I can see Serenity is eager to tell you more, so I will let her explain and come back to you soon.

After Pyre appeared, I walked towards Tarum and Rista. We all hugged and said our goodbyes. They both told me to stay safe and to send word if I located Tarum's other friends. I agreed and prepared myself, tied on my cape, and connected my staff to my belt so that when I was airborne it would not fall.

Knowing my flight would be a long one, I walked back to my dragon, who lowered himself so I could step on him. After getting a good grip on his neck and shoulders, and waving once more to my friends, I pushed off my mount and, with a burst of speed, was soon away from Mirrorwood, the temple, and my friends. Realising it had been a while since I had been alone, I set my mind to finding help. Thanks, Tarum, back to you. I will return to my part soon.

Thanks, Serenity. We all hope that everything would go well for you. Now I know you are eager to find out how Blade and Magna got on, so let me leave you for now, and I will let Blade tell you, their story.

Brightleaf Day 4

Hi all, Blade the warrior here. I know, you people are so lucky, so let's tell our story. Of course, we all know the real hero of it.

Not knowing what trouble our two comrades were facing, Magna and I made our way to Graven Vale Hollow, as we knew from past adventures that it was one place that had a large, evil connection.

We both tried to approach Graven Vale Hollow but, as we did, a rancid gas surrounded it. The gas had a horrible effect on us both and left us feeling woozy and confused.

After a few hours, when our heads had finally cleared, we followed another path and came into a different village, the sign indicating that it was called Purestrom. Once there, the place looked quite eerie. The streets were empty, and the light was so poor that we could only just make out a tavern and a few small stalls. We also saw a healer's house, instantly recognising it by the familiar sign of a medicine bottle outside it.

Feeling very thirsty, we found our way to the tavern. Unlike the street, this place was filled with powerful trolls and ugly-looking demons. We both realised that we had been led into a trap probably set by Mysi. Luckily, we had an advantage,

I had my trusty sword in my hand and, unbeknown to the creatures my good friend Magna could prepare spells faster than all other wizards.

I was first to strike, and I used my pure muscle to flip a table over to get the troll's attention. It had the desired effect, and I was now fighting a huge and burly troll. I love a good scrap and was in my element. I looked over and saw Magna had decided magic was the answer, no surprise there.

I watched him cast a mighty *Auraa* spell. A large, purple mist enveloped some of the demons and trolls, and they froze where they stood still in their attack poses.

I took full advantage of this moment and struck down the troll I was fighting, and then two more trolls, and a demon that had been struck by the spell. The downside was, because it was such a powerful spell, I could see Magna stumble around. I knew he was now vulnerable to attack and, as I was in mid battle with a multi-armed, sword-wielding demon, I couldn't get to him. I finally defeated the demon and watched as the few survivors fled out of the tavern.

Once the chaos had ended, I looked for Magna. I finally located him, spotting him on the other side of the room bleeding badly on the floor near an overturned table. I ran to my best friend and felt for a pulse. I found a shallow one, and I knew that I must find help urgently. I grabbed Magna carefully and, using my remaining strength, dragged him outside, avoiding the various hazards of our earlier battle but leaving a trail of the mage's blood wherever we went.

Back on the street, the lanterns in some windows had been lit. In the new light, I located a nearby bench and laid Magna on it. I began hunting for help but first, I patched him up by making a temporary tourniquet, using a bit of my shirt, to stem the bleeding. It worked for a while, but I knew he needed medical help as soon as possible.

Once on the bench, I saw Magna had taken a turn for the worse; he was now shivering violently. I then remembered seeing the healer's house and decided to try to find it. I regretfully left my friend and retraced our earlier path. After walking around, I finally managed to reach the healer's house.

I knocked on the door, but no one answered. I was about to walk away, then I heard a light creak and, looking back, noticed the door was now slightly ajar. Thinking it might be another trap, but not worried about of my own safety only Magna's health, I entered the poorly lit house and was immediately confronted by a tall, thin shadow.

I could see the shadow was armed, as a glint of silver could occasionally be seen. The shadow began lashing out, determined to protect their home which i didn't hold it against them as in their position I would of done the same. A few jabs struck me, but I shrugged them off, just more scars to add to my ever-growing collection, more scars to show my adoring female fans.

The figure pushed me towards the door and then, without warning, my whole body stopped moving, I couldn't speak, move, or even blink. I knew that a spell had been used on me. As the shadow reached to light the torch, the room was revealed.

I saw it was much larger than it looked, shelves of medical texts and scrolls of magic filled the walls, and potion bottles and healing apparatus were locked in big, wooden cabinets.

In the new light, my eyes followed around the room to find the figure. To my surprise, it was actually a young-looking elf. I tried to speak but couldn't. Now I was worried, my friend was hurt badly and I couldn't move or talk. The elf seemed to be sizing me up. After what seem like ages but was probably just a few minutes, I felt the spell leave me. Slowly, my arms and legs became less stiff, as I felt my body wake up. I tried speaking. Gradually, and with much effort, I managed it, and I began to explain why I had come and that I needed the healer's help.

I hated asking for help, because from a young age I had always handled everything on my own; having absent parents gives you no choice in that.

As I spoke, I saw the elf listen intently. I hoped he would soon trust me, as the longer it took the more, I worried for Magna.

Eventually, the elf introduced himself as Telim Zek. He went on to explain his reason for protecting himself. It turned out his wife Helen and her pet dragon Shadow had been abducted at knifepoint. In return for helping Magna, I offered to find out more about Helen and Shadow's location.

Telim agreed, he then grabbed his bag of medical supplies and followed me back out of his house. After locking it, we quickly walked through the town to where we found Magna who had rolled off the bench and was unconscious on the floor. I saw Telim use a small healing spell to stop the bleeding and then re-dressed my friend's wound. He stuffed the bloody piece of shirt I'd used earlier into a empty bag.

Both of us then helped Magna back to the house. Telim manoeuvred to unlock the door, we went into his bedroom and laid Magna on the double bed. After a close examination, Telim told me that Magna had been struck by a venomous Lifi demon's weapon. This weapon was coated with a potent poison known as Dementioa.

He then explained this powerful toxin could cause paralysis, blood poisoning and, in higher enough doses, death. The only cure for it was a concoction of black scale liquid, and he explained this was why his wife and her dragon had been abducted.

Only when Helen and he worked together and using Shadows scales could the mixture be made, so Mysi was using Helen to force Telim to do his bidding, but so far, he had refused, as that was what his wife admired about him, his resolve.

Telim told me how a horde of demons had torn people from their houses and dragged them away in chains with plans to infect them with the Dementioa, so that Mysi could enslave them more easily. Angry at this abuse of power, I asked Telim if I could leave my friend in his care and how I could be advised of Magna's condition.

Telim handed me a pure white stone and explained that it portrayed phantom images of whoever was contacting you. It was called an elven contact stone and, due to the size, they were the best way of communicating throughout most continents. He went on to explain that if the stone began glowing someone was trying to reach me, as many people used this form of communication.

I thanked Telim and left him some Xens for Magna's upkeep. After a few hours' rest and trying not to think about my best friend's condition, I left the village upset and now alone. I reached the end of the road but, to my horror, found that I was now standing on the edge of a tree-lined cliff, the previous methods of crossing now all fallen away, and I now knew that the next town of Trollstone was only accessible by air. With no way to get there, had my journey already come to an end?

Trying not to worry, I looked to the sky and that was when I saw a huge shadow getting closer. I drew my trusty sword in no mood for yet another fight but, as the shadow got closer, I saw a vibrant red flash which belonged to a large scarlet dragon that was heading straight for me.

Knowing a sword couldn't stop a dragon and with no potions and unable to cast magic, I quickly looked for cover and found a small cave. I ran inside, just as I felt a massive blast of hot wind. I could see the trees swaying back and forth in the downdraught of wind as the mighty beast landed just on the edge of the cliff.

From the dragon's back stepped the most beautiful woman I had ever seen, and I had seen and dated a few women, let me tell you. She was holding an ornate, red staff and attached to her shoulders was a flowing cape made of fire.

I've always loved to show off for a powerful woman, and I felt drawn to her. I decided to leave the cave and walked towards her. She did not seem impressed, so I began flexing my large muscles which always made the ladies swoon. The woman was just staring in disbelief at my attempt to woo her. I had never had this happen and was shocked by her response.

I soon regretted my decision because, as I got too close to the lady to try one more flirtation, her dragon sent forth a massive blast of fire which narrowly missed me and cremated a nearby bush.

Hi all, it's me, Serenity. Let me tell you how I felt at this guy's failed romantic attempt and why he nearly became a dead man; as if someone of my skill and feminine wiles would look twice at him.

After many attempts, I managed to calm down my beast and bid the foolish warrior approach. I asked him outright if he knew of a young elf called Tarum and waited on his response, knowing that if I didn't like it, we would fry him. Luckily for him, he said yes, he had travelled with him and they were good friends. Not sure if I could trust him, I also asked his name, and he proudly said, Blade the Masterful. After introducing myself, I explained about Tarum and Rista but was puzzled, as Tarum had told me that Blade would be accompanied by Magna the Great, who I had always admired as a sort of hero.

When I asked Blade about Magna, to my surprise, this strong warrior showed a different side. He became sad and his disheartened voice went on to explain about their fight and Magna's illness. Shocked by his story, and having heard of other victims dying from Dementioa, I agreed to take him to Trollstone but asked that we make a stop in a village called **Mirrioa**, but first I updated Tarum on my progress by borrowing Blade's new contact stone. He was pleased I was safe and clearly shocked by Magna's illness.

He didn't know the real reason I wanted to visit was to try to find out more information on my father and why he'd vanished, as this village was the last place he had been seen by one of my mum's Druid friends.

I knew that warriors didn't have much experience with riding dragons, they normally just slaughtered them as proof of their skill. Well, he now had a choice; stay on the cliff or fly with me on a monstrous beast. Thankfully, he decided to travel with me. I introduced my steed as Pyre and, after watching how I mounted him, he followed hesitantly. Much to my horror, he put his arms around my waist for security; an arrangement only he was happy with.

Once we were safely aboard, I instructed Pyre to sink to the ground then, with a huge rush and away from the cliff s, I shot him up as if we had just been fired by a catapult. Blade had, at this time, turned a dark jade colour. This made me smile; I would show him I was no one's prize.

Soon we were soaring through the clouds and over high mountains. Once he was airborne, I discovered that the journey wasn't so bad for Blade and he began to enjoy it. After a while, I got Pyre to descend, as a great forest came into view. I then explained to Blade that somewhere in that huge forest there was the village of Mirrioa. I told him to stay close to me, because the villagers didn't like non-magic users, as they felt all should have a basic knowledge of magic.

As I had seen a more emotional side of him, I decided to tell Blade about my father and his disappearance. Once we had landed in a nearby clearing, I cast a *Transform* spell and Pyre became a beautiful red jewel which I placed onto my staff.

Blade and I headed down a muddy path into the thick forest. The ground was wet from recent rainfall and the trees were dark shades of green, hardly any light could penetrate them. As we got deeper, I could see a clearing and some flat stones set in a circle. We were both tired after our flight, so we set up a small camp within the stones using the wood and leaves nearby, and we were both soon asleep. Unbeknown to us, while we slept something special happened. The moon was now high and, as the moonbeams shone on the stones, it awakened the slumbering terrain magic within them and the ground was shaking heavily. We were so exhausted that we slept on, not realising that the stones had risen and cut off any escape and now left us trapped, as we had unknowingly awoken **Mystic Henge**.

When I awoke, I was awestruck, and I realised that both Blade and I were now caught in a ring of glowing stones.

I woke Blade and, on seeing the stones, he was as shocked as me. While we were devising a way out of our predicament, the glowing on the stones began to get brighter.

When the glow had faded, a group of ghostly, golden human archers and wizards surrounded us. One of the ghosts, a much broader elf, was wearing a large, long cloak and on his head was an imposing crown, while he stood a little away from his army.

As soon as the ghosts had surrounded us, I saw Blade grab his sword, and as he did this the archers fired back in defence. Luckily, I was quick enough to cast a *Bright Dome* spell. The arrows hit the white, magic shield that now covered us and they bounced off. As we defended ourselves from the onslaught of arrows, we saw the cloaked elf make his way towards us. He walked straight through the dome as if it was nothing more than an open door, and we were now confronted by a large angry spirit who was pointing his staff towards us in a warning manner.

We knew this confrontation would either help or hinder us. The cloaked ghost then called out a command, and his army stood to attention awaiting further orders; it was very clear that this elf was a king.

I remembered to follow the rules of meeting monarchs that I had learnt from my mum, so I bowed then held out my hand as a sign of respect. The king looked puzzled but, after a few minutes, he pointed his staff away and smiled. Seeming grateful that some remembered the old ways, we listened to him.

His voice was very deep and powerful with an deep earth tone, and I could tell by the tone this king was respected. The elf introduced himself as Lichen the Mighty and his tribe as Woodlins. He explained that he and his army had perished at these stones so their spirits were trapped there. My concern had ebbed, and I introduced myself and Blade. Lichen explained to us that we had stumbled on to Mystic Henge, a powerful, magical place that had been guarded against evil for centuries as it could harness great power if awoken on a certain day, and this power could magnify any element of magic including Darc and Poison. The king then asked why we had entered his domain.

I explained about our quest for the sphere and saw the king thinking something over, the power the artefact contained. He agreed to let us pass by and ordered his army to withdraw. One by one, the golden army vanished into the stones which slowly sank back into the earth releasing us.

The king, who was the last to leave, explained that the entrance to Mirrioa was well concealed in a thick forest that was not what it seemed. Then, after giving us a royal wave and wishing us well, he too faded.

We left the stones more informed; I couldn't believe I had encountered a race of my ancestors and wished I had asked more questions. I was determined to ask Lightning about Mystic Henge, as I thought maybe with its added power we could help our land. We carried on down another path where the forest grew much deeper.

The light cast strange shadows around us, and I was sure I heard footsteps behind me. Sure enough, after a few more steps, we were both surrounded by a pack of little, brown, imp-like creatures who could only been seen when they moved, as their cloaks blended perfectly to their surroundings making it evident that these Cloaken were ambush hunters.

Both of us were surprised by their appearance from the quiet forest around us, but we were soon prepared for battle.

OK adventurers, it's my turn to show you the real power of this warrior. Here's my next part of the story.

Two of the Cloaken leapt at me ready to attack with their poisoned blades. Their blows hit me before I could react, sending two shots of venom into my arm. Ignoring the pain, I fought back and soon my attackers were dead, beside their bodies their weapons tinged with my blood.

I saw Serenity was also being attacked. Knowing she could handle herself; I watched impressed as she fought off the Cloaken using her staff and she managed to burn some by sweeping her fiery cloak around unleashing small flames. She must have known that these creatures were known to be highly magic resistant as she defended herself from their poisoned blades.

Finally, after a long fight and once out of the woods, I felt the poison passing through my blood causing my arm to blister, and I also felt very lethargic. Within minutes, I had slumped to the ground.

Thank you, great warrior, for your input. Now, as you were incapacitated, can I carry on with the story? Many thanks.

I knew I had to get help, so I banged hard on a large wooden gate that seemed to appear from the forest itself. Hoping that it was Mirrioa, as I had never been lucky enough to find it, I knocked again as hard as I could.

Eventually, I heard the echo of chanting voices, and a few moments later the gate opened to reveal a beautiful, human woman who had long, auburn hair, bright, hazel eyes and
 she carried a silver staff.

Luckily for me she was friendly and introduced herself as Zelena Starlight, and she went on to explain she was the current head sorceress of Mirrioa. I smiled to myself; I had finally found it. After listening to her, I introduced us and asked if the city had a healer or a clinic as my friend outside had been stabbed with Cloaken weapons.

Zelena told me they only had a single cure for Cloaken venom, as it was quite common for her people to get attacked living so close to the vile creatures, but that it could only be used during the midnight hour for that was when the blessed orchid bloomed.

With this new information, Zelena and I brought Blade into the village. Zelena closed the gates and sealed them with a powerful *Invisible Dome* spell. I knew this was a great way to guard the village from both the Cloaken and outsiders, and I was grateful to have been allowed access.

Zelena then took us both to the temple. She handed me a map of Mirrioa, she also offered to let us have something to eat and a room. Once I had settled Blade down in the small room attached to the temple, and eaten a small meal of fruit and bread, Zelena guided me around her village. I asked about my father. She said she had no information on him but would keep her ear out in case she heard anything. As we wandered around, I could see how beautiful it was. Large stone buildings lined the streets, up and down, that were all covered with colourful flowers, and there were many shops and stalls to tempt the few visitors who came or the locals that lived there. One place stood out to me. It was called **Hatchers' Paradise**, and the reason I noticed it was the dragon symbol that was attached to the sign above the door.

The head sorceress explained that this store was owned and run by Lunar Majestic, a local dragon tamer trying to help change people's perception of dragons. She then bid me goodbye to go and prepare her tools to help prune the blessed orchid, as Zelena wished me well and headed back towards the temple, excited, I walked into the shop and began to browse. As I moved towards the hatchery, a young elven woman came towards me. The woman introduced herself as Lunar Majestic, daughter of Seliza Majestic. She seemed to have a natural likeability and put me at ease straight away, so I went on to explain about being a qualified dragon protector and ember mistress and about our journey so far including Blade's attack.

We had a long conversation and, once we had finished, Lunar said she felt an affinity with me and, to my pleasant surprise, offered to let me adopt a dragon. I was thrilled so, one by one, I examined all the eggs in the hatchery. Th re were lots to choose from, large brown spiky ones, bright yellow grooved ones, and huge pointed red ones, but I finally chose a deeply grooved blue one. It was shaped like a raindrop and stood out from the bunch,after holding it in my hands I got a tingling feeling all over.

Lunar came over and asked if I had realised that I was now glowing slightly? She recognised I had a natural gift with dragons, just like herself and her mum, and I was so overwhelmed to be told this.

She then went on to explain that she would send the dragon egg to her mum in Volcania using a *Portal* spell. This was the safest mode of transport, more reliable for the egg, with less chance of damage, and she carried on to say that raising dragons needed a particular skill that her mum alone possessed.

Lunar then cast a powerful *Bond* spell on the egg. Knowing I was now connected to this dragon, I understood that as I grew and developed so would it.

She told me, as the dragon matured, it would know that I would be its mistress. I named my future dragon Ripple, then saw her admiring my dragon pendant, and I explained how I had got it.

Lunar was very impressed by my encounter with our land's guardian and offered to add a contact stone to my pendant, so I could be updated on my dragon's progress. I agreed, pleased with the help Lunar had offered. Now my new dragon pendant was infused with great intensity and had a warm and loving glow.

With a new dragon egg to focus on, I thanked my new friend and readied to return to the temple as, in my haste conversing with Lunar about dragons, I had forgotten how long I had been away from Blade.

It was now just gone midnight. I made my way back to the temple and noticed the buildings were now dark, all except for the one I needed. On entering the temple, I saw Zelena wearing pure white, silk gloves which held a stunning flower that had a mauve light. Drawing my eyes away from the flower, I then saw Blade. He looked a lot worse than before; his arm had swollen and he was shaking violently.

Shocked by how quick his condition had worsened; I asked Zelena how the flower would help. The sorceress told me that this was the blessed orchid, a rare and unique flower grown only in the forest that surrounded Mirrioa. By collecting the nectar from the flower and capturing the mauve glow, she could create the antidote to the Cloaken venom.

Zelena said the only downside was, once the cure had taken effect, it would paralyse Blade until the poison had left his bloodstream, and this could take days or weeks or possibly years depending on the dose of venom.

I knew I had to press on with my adventure and try to locate Helen and Shadow in an effort to help Magna overcome the Dementioa poison, so I asked Zelena to look after Blade until he was cured, and I would also leave some Xens for his upkeep. Zelena agreed and offered to send a warrior from the city to accompany me, as it was very dangerous outside the city for a lady alone.

I hated the thought of journeying with someone else, as I had just started to see Blade differently but, so not to be rude, I accepted her offer.

Zelena then left, only to come back a few hours later with a strong, burly human warrior known as Silver Sword. He looked quite young with his short, brown hair and athletic build, and he had a familiar resemblance to someone I had travelled with, but I couldn't think of where or how I knew him. I was wiped out, and I said goodnight to Zelena and Silver in the morning, Silver and I washed, ate and then checked on Blade. I saw a look of confusion pass across Silver's face, as he looked at Blade, but thought nothing of it.

I found Zelena was not around and surmised that she must be in town sorting stuff out. Once on the street, Lunar came running towards us. After she had caught her breath, she told us that her mother had contacted her because dragons had been sighted in the **Great Ice Plains** and the surrounding area. I knew this was unusual as, apart from certain species, most dragons hated the cold.

I also knew I must find these magnificent beasts; after asking Lunar how far the Great Ice Plains were from our current location. She told us that they could be found far in the west and that we would need to fly there, as no road covered the area, due to its treacherous landscape and its hostile creatures.

I knew that the plains would be cold so, from the local store, I invested in a hooded jacket made from Chillern hare fur and Silver, having visited the plains before, bought some more winter mail he could wear underneath his armour. With our purchased clothes packed into my bag.

Lunar showed us to a flat piece of land where I summoned my mighty pet Chill from his jewel. Silver Sword and I clambered aboard my great beast. I was impressed how secure he was around dragons, something most warriors felt was beneath them, and, after making sure our bags and equipment were safe, we flew into the clear, blue sky.

I saw how much Chill was pleased to be back in the air, he was showing off for his new passenger by flying fast, then diving, then turning sharply. Both of us were confident flyers and enjoyed every trick, and before we knew it the Great Ice Plains appeared below us; huge mountains, jagged and sharp, that looked like some great monster's teeth.

My dragon came into land on a small, flat piece of land between two of the huge mountains.

Once off the dragon, our feet began crunching on the snowy ground, and we also put on our warm clothes. Soon, we had begun trekking through the snow. Icy cold winds were blowing snow everywhere, so it was hard to see. Also, as the night drew in, the temperature dropped quickly. Soon we had no choice and were forced to find shelter in an old, abandoned cave. Chill was in his element and stood guard outside, while we used brute strength and magic inside the cave and soon had a roaring fire going. We were both getting hungry so began to forage in the cave. We rustled up a meal of roasted bat and had Chillern berries for dessert.

Hunger sated, we began to try and relax, but sitting on a cave floor that was muddy and cold wasn't exactly relaxing, though at least we were warm.

Once we were safe and fed, Chill went hunting and managed to catch a few Chillern hares, then returned to his post and began to eat his prey, while the two of us slept.

Refreshed and ready to carry on, we resumed our trek through the inhospitable land, until we came to a large, frozen lake. We thought to cross it by foot but, just as I stepped onto it, Chill pushed me back onto solid ground. I had no idea why Chill was acting so strange.

Then, looking across the lake, I found out why his behaviour was not normal; a threat had arrived. We saw a large horde of Frostling's appear on the opposite bank. These reptilian creatures were small but deadly. They were at home in the icy terrain and could cross the ice with ease. Soon, a mass of scales and claws were charging towards us ready to kill.

Chill stood in front of us, and the swarm clambered all over my dragon, biting and clawing. I knew he was greatly outnumbered and, after a brave battle, my dragon withdrew. He was covered in scratches, bite marks, and a deep gash on his neck, and I watched him skulk away. As much as it hurt to see Chill injured, he had given me and Silver time to prepare, and we stood side by side ready to defend ourselves.

I was first to act casting my *Flaming Arrow* spell and managed to knock out a few with it. When the spell hit their frozen bodies, they melted before my eyes. Silver meanwhile had managed to kill some more but, even though their pack had lost members, the Frostling's still carried on. After a fierce and long, drawn-out battle, we headed out to look for our injured friend.

To my horror, I finally found him. In fact, he was just a few metres ahead of where the battle had happened, but he was lying motionless on the snow which was now blood red. I ran towards Chill with tears in my eyes. When I got to him, his breath was very shallow and I knew if I didn't try and help him, he would die.

I tried a spell I had never used, but I knew it was the only chance my dragon had, so I cast *Repair Wounds*. Soon my body became encased in a blue glow. As I touched my injured friend, the light left my body and began to snake around the dragon. Tendrils of magic wrapped around him like a large cocoon, and after just a few minutes the glow faded but, to my surprise, nothing happened. I had failed. I began to shudder and weep, as tears flooded my already red cheeks and splashed onto the snowy ground. Silver tried to comfort me, but I pushed him away, then I just fell to floor broken-hearted next to my dragon.

I began to gently rub his scales, as I did this he began to shudder. Terrified at what was happening, I reluctantly fled away. Hours passed, but I refused to believe my friend was gone, so I stayed with my mighty beast but kept a safe distance. After another hour, and fighting to stay awake, Silver insisted I could do no more for my dragon, plus the wind was picking up and the beast had not moved.

I grudgingly agreed, walked carefully towards my brave friend where, after pressing my hand to his scales one last time, I felt his final breath. My scaly friend had passed, and the tears once again began to sting my eyes, as I left my friend alone in the cold, desolate landscape. We both walked away, as the guilt began to consume us. We couldn't believe Chill had been killed just for protecting us.

We then made our way back to the lake and decided between us how best to cross it. Knowing that Chill's death would be avenged, with this new resolve we began coming up with a way to cross the lake. Realising that if we couldn't pass it our journey would end, I decided to use my magma magic to melt the ice and then we both thought we might be able to swim across it. So, I walked to the edge of the lake and touched my staff to it. The ice began to slowly melt, but now a new problem arose; the water underneath was flowing too fast and it was freezing cold, we could not swim it. Silver had found another way to cross the vast lake, but it was very dangerous. He pointed towards some large, flat stones that were scattered on its surface which had been revealed when the ice melted. It was our only way over, and we began the laborious task of crossing.

We could not rush it, though, as our feet kept slipping, plus the wind kept threatening to topple us into the icy depths. After many hours, we had finally crossed the treacherous lake. Once across, we trekked on until we reached an old, decrepit hut that had apparently belong to someone. The door was ajar and, on closer examination, the old fi replace had been recently lit.

Silver stood guard outside, while I made the hut more liveable. I relit the fire using my magma magic and found some old, moth-eaten blankets which I draped on the floor. Even though it wasn't what we were used to, we made ourselves at home.

We were exhausted after our long, emotional journey, so we settled down to sleep. As I was drifting off, my amulet began glowing. I opened it to see an unknown elf's face appear. He seemed as shocked as I was and, after realising that he was not talking to Blade, he introduced himself as Telim and asked about Blade. I introduced myself and explained about Blade's condition. He went on to inform me that Magna was doing well but was not ready to participate in our quest. After agreeing to pass on the information, the image vanished and the glowing stone went cold.

Unbeknown to us, while we slept, we were no longer alone. In the dead of night, a shadowy figure had slipped quietly into the hut unnoticed.

Brightleaf Day 5

I awoke and started to collect my things. To my amazement, I turned around and there was my friend Lightning, standing by the door in her human guise.

Just as I was going to find out why Lightning was there, Silver awoke and, noticing a stranger in the hut, he stood in front of me, sword ready to protect me. I was impressed with the brave act and thought back to the weird look that he gave Blade, and I surmised that he and Blade must be brothers.

Hi all, Lightning again. I hope you are enjoying this story so far.

I was impressed with the new warrior's bravery and introduced myself and my position to him. He acted startled at this revelation, but he also remained silent. I didn't know why, but he just stared at me.

Serenity explained to me about Chill's demise. She hoped I could resurrect the great beast, but I refused, explaining that I was banned from using my abilities to help someone cheat death; it was one of my father's unbreakable rules.

Angry at my refusal, something changed in Serenity. I felt her power grow, the rage and sadness inside her began to seep through her veins, and she was now a vivid red colour. I worried for Silver's life and, using my strength, dragged him away. Still protesting about his friend, we got out of the hut and as far away as possible.

It was just in time, as seconds later a powerful explosion ripped through the shelter and turned it to cinders. The ground shook and there in the inferno, with fire whirling around her, Serenity remained unharmed but anger personified.

The power reminded me of when my own guardian powers had fully developed and materialised.

ok, and with that, I will hand back to my heroes; I needed time to recover. Back to Serenity.

I was dazed and confused. I just remember stumbling teary-eyed out of the remains of the hut and fell to my knees on the cold snow, then darkness.

When I awoke, I wasn't on the ground any more, Lightning had gone, and I found myself in a larger hut. An open fire burned a few inches away, and the walls were covered in traps of all shapes and sizes.

There was a little sink in the corner of the hut. I soon began to feel better, but then the tragedy that I had recently gone through came flooding back into my head, tears once again stung my face, and my head throbbed. I finally calmed down, got myself to together and decided to wash my face. As I splashed the water, the cold helped me a lot. As I was just drying my face on an old towel, I saw a familiar face.

Silver walked towards me. He told me that he had helped carry me here, and I felt a wave of relief envelop me along with his warm embrace. I remembered, even though I had lost someone, people still cared for me and I was not alone in my task.

I was even closer to him now and the resemblance to Blade was much clearer, the same dark hair and the same brave and caring attitude. I soon felt better and left the large hut, and I saw that I had been brought to a settler's camp with lot of strange races gathered around a tree stump.

Intrigued, I joined the crowd, and I began to smile as I saw another familiar face. Holding a dark blue drakeling on her lap sat my good friend Lunar. I was puzzled. How had she known to journey to the camp? But she explained that she had been sent another message by her mum and had travelled using a *Portal* spell. I was both surprised and shocked at how my egg had developed, as Lunar had not updated me like she said she would. On seeing Silver and I, Lunar got up and carried the baby dragon to us. Lunar handed me the baby, apologised to me and went on to explain how the *Portal* spell she'd used had caused the dragon to grow quicker than others, that's why she hadn't spoken to me. Its spiky, little tail curled around my finger, and I stroked its head as it fell asleep in my arms. Ripple and I had now been reunited.

Lunar saw that I had been crying and asked why. Holding back more tears, I explained what had befallen Chill. Lunar was in shock as, like her mum, she had always cared and looked after the dragons throughout the lands. She just stood and wept with me. Silver put his arm around Lunar and led her to the large hut followed by a tearful me and Ripple, but as she was so young I decided to leave Ripple in the hut, so I placed Ripple on a stool in the building. She was still fast asleep, snoring quietly, as we left.

Hi everyone, I'm Silver, nice to meet you I am a warrior from a small town my story is for another time but let's just say I have a reason for questing, so let carry this on shall we

I noticed someone else was now present in the hut, a young, elven lady was putting a small, blue lizard in a cage. I knew she was a huntress, as she wore padded gauntlets, a fur cape, and some lightweight boots. She looked to be about twenty-five which was unusual, as most hunters I had seen were older and male. Serenity seemed interested in discovering more about the lizard. I saw her walk next to the lady and I followed. On closer examination, the cage held a lizard that resembled a Frostling which might have been a cross-breed of the same two species. Due to the look of the creature, Serenity was once again reminded of recent events and she fled the large hut in tears.

I saw the lady turn. She was shocked at Serenity's response to her newly caught skinkling and pushed past me, running after Serenity.

Thanks, Silver. So here we go again, I seem to talk a lot. Sorry about that.

The lady found me huddled under a bare tree sobbing loudly. She walked softly towards me and sat down next to me introducing herself as Mallim. Then explained how she had found me unconscious and, with the help of the humans and others, she had managed to get me to the camp.

I slowly calmed myself down and told her my name and the story so far, including why I was so upset.

I then asked Mallim if she knew of a place called **Mitra**, as I knew we needed to head there to relax after our long and emotional journey. Mallim went on to tell me that it was her local city; she had been born and raised there. She offered to help Silver and me get there, but told me the journey was going to be tough, as we would encounter many different and dangerous creatures, and that it would take us several hours.

We walked back to Mallim's hut and found Silver. Once Mallim had apologised, and they had made their introductions, our trio prepared for the long journey. I gathered my things along with Ripple.

I got Lunar's attention and asked her if she would like to join us, as I knew her expertise with dragons would be invaluable. She agreed, so we made sure to prepare extra for our travels and then left the camp.

I knew Ripple was very precious, so I cast a *Transform* spell on her turning her into a small, blue diamond. I placed her in my cloak pocket; she would be much safer there. Once out of the camp, the wind and snow had ebbed slightly but, as the ground was still quite icy and dangerous, our progress was slow.

Mallim led the way, with her sword held high, keeping a safe distance between us all, then came Silver, followed by Lunar and then me. In a chain format, we all knew that we had less chance of being ambushed.

We carried on walking, until we found a small path that had been carved out of the ice. We all stepped on the track and heard our feet crunch. Thinking it was just ice, we didn't bother looking, but my curiosity got the better of me and, as we came to solid ground, I looked back at why the ground was crunching. To my horror, it was not ice but scattered animal bones.

As we travelled, I felt my contact stone glowing so, turning my pendant around, I saw an older woman's face appear. This person was not recognisable at first, but I realised she had a striking resemblance to Lunar. Her image began speaking, she introduced herself as Seliza Majestic and, I was right, she was Lunar's mum. When Lunar came over to explain about us being in the Great Ice Plains, Seliza seemed puzzled and she said that she had not sent a message, as she was busy with **Strong Wings**, her dragon training school, and had not used her contact stone for days. I could see Lunar go quiet; I knew something was wrong. Hi all. Sorry, Serenity, but I need to explain how I felt. My name is Lunar in the princess of Volcania and help my mother and my aunt at her dragon training academy but as you know from earlier most of the time, I run my shop.

Guilt tore through me; I had led my friends to this place and a mighty beast had fallen. Serenity spoke to me and reassured me that I was not to blame and life happens, friends pass, and life moves on.

Feeling better, I was soon back to my old, happy self. OK, back to our ember mistress. Sorry it was so short, but you'll hear from me again, I'm sure.

Once the message had been given, Seliza's face vanished and the stone went cold. I didn't tell Mallim, as she was too far ahead. We made our way closer to the huntress so not to get lost. As we all reached her, Mallim had stopped and was listening to the wind. Then we all heard it, an ominous, ear-splitting howl cut the air.

Suddenly, out of the snowy wind, a huge monster came charging towards us. As it got closer, we saw that a Horngor had us in its sights. I knew these massive beasts were the top predator of the plains. They were covered in thick, white and blue shaggy fur and had two huge horns that could tear flesh in an instant.

I saw that Mallim had thrown a bola at the beast, but her aim was slightly off and it missed by a few metres. I saw Lunar knew exactly what to do next. She told us to gather together and then cast *Lite Dome*, and I was so pleased to see a barrier of light shimmer around our group. The beast ran straight into it, which caused it to become dazed and confused, and we all cheered as it starting charging away from us. Knowing that the spell wouldn't hold that long, we sped up our trek and soon arrived outside Mitra, just as the familiar pop of the dome fading could be heard.

Mallim made her way to the gate. We all followed, but something was odd. A strange symbol had been gouged into the gate, and we gasped in shock as we realised the symbol was a bloody hand. Mallim drew her sword, spoke an incantation, then followed the lines of the symbol with her sword. As she did this, a strange, mauve light snaked all around it tracing its shape, she then placed her hand on the symbol and pushed the gate open.

Mitra was a massive city; unlike the previous ones we had visited; it was the biggest city so far of the journey. From the entrance, it had loads of winding paths leading to many large, neglected buildings that had ivy growing around them and parts of the buildings were crumbling. Mallim led us to the large town square. I could Lunar and the others were on edge. I guessed we all felt the same way as wherever we went people would be smiling eerily. I was longing to leave this place, and now, something about Mallim seemed odd.

Maybe it was the city and not the guide that was making me nervous. Mallim led us past a dirty, old tavern with a cracked sign. We could just make out the name, it was called **The Smoking Witch**, and further along we saw a weird shop that showed chains, and whips, and masks, then we saw the store was called **Slaves and Staffs**. Lunar stuck close to me, as we made our way to another tavern known as **Mortals' Coil**.

I saw Lunar was now terrified and I could see why. This building looked like someone had stuck it together with glue, the door was battered, the windows were smashed, and bits of wood were splitting, making the wood look like a huge Arania had been spinning its web across it.

Hello people, it's me Silver. Let me carry on the story and give Serenity a break.

We entered and saw lots of humans. Most were scared or looked drugged, but some were dressed in black and carried long, leather whips. I vowed, if I had to, I would add more scars and protect my friends. I asked Mallim about the patrons of the inn, but she just hurried towards the bar with Lunar and Serenity.

Once at the bar, Mallim left us. I found she had begun chatting to an ogre-sized man about rooms. All the while the patrons of the inn were showing anger, they cracked their knuckles, and the men were leering at the woman like lions getting ready to pounce. I hoped that no one tried anything because, if they did, the predator would become the prey, as I knew the women would be more than a match for them. I could see both women were nervous, as they kept glancing around the tavern as we all chatted and agreed that this place was dangerous and just like an open bear trap it could snap shut at any time.

Sometime later, Mallim returned, but kept looking in any direction except at us, and explained that she had paid for the best rooms in the inn for tonight and that tomorrow we would explore the town.

Serenity seemed ok, but both Lunar and I just said thanks in an unconvincing way. Mallim told us our rooms were upstairs, so we traipsed up the threadbare, carpeted stairs hearing every creak and crack. I was worried that they might just give way and crumble sending us toppling back to the ground level.

When I got to my room, I wished I could have slept outside as, on closer expectation, I was in a small box room with a wooden floor that had rotted in places, causing a rancid smell in the air. The room had just a few items of furniture in it. A broken wardrobe dominated most of the room, and I could just make out the chipped paint on one of the doors that used to be red with a slight golden edge.

My place to wash, not that I would ever use it, was a leaky, old sink filled with a strange, green liquid that was dripping onto the wooden floor. The bed was four bits of wood, two sides, one bottom and one chipped headboard, which contained just a filthy mattress. The only consolation was that I wasn't planning on staying in this pit of a room, I was going to find out what the weird town was hiding. Once night had fallen, I made my way out of the room onto the landing, which was slightly illuminated thanks to some wall lights that were trying their hardest to stay on. This gave me some excellent cover, as it cast quite good shadows that I could use to make my way downstairs.

I crept along to the ladies' room and saw that their door was closed. I was just coming back, when I heard heavy footsteps. Ducking back in the shadows, a pair of furred boots walked right past me, and I realised someone else was wide awake. I then followed the steps, being careful not to be seen, and made my way to the stairs. I took my time walking down the stairs. When I reached the ground floor, the pub was now empty. I used the shadows some more and then hid under a table. The boots were heading for the door. I felt a slight shiver as the door opened, then, making sure to get through it before it closed, I appeared outside. The city was deathly quiet and poorly lit. I heard another set of footsteps coming from my left-hand side. I turned to face to the left but, as I did, the world went black.

Brightleaf Day 6

Once I awoke, I felt terrible. A pounding headache threatened to consume me, I also felt ropes that bound my hands. I struggled as best I could, but the ropes didn't budge.

I tried to ignore the pain in my head and get my bearings. I found out I was tied to a chair. I saw the room was unloved; cobwebs and dust coated nearly everywhere. I then felt a tickling on my leg. When I looked down, I was shocked, as a gigantic, brown rat began making its way up it. I shook my leg the best I could and managed to get rid of it, but not before it got its revenge by biting me and scratching. As I managed to shake it off, it flew from my leg and ran back into the shadows.

Feeling pain, I looked down and noticed that the bite mark had started bleeding. Slowly, I felt the sting as the blood trickled down my leg. Knowing that I couldn't stop the bleeding with my hands bound, I used all my remaining strength and managed to topple the chair. Now that the chair was on its side, I managed to get a better grip on the ropes and, after several minutes, was finally loose.

My leg was now agony, and to my horror, the blood that had leaked from the wound was now running faster. My whole lower leg was stained red and the pain intensified. I hobbled as best I could, but had only got a little way before my leg collapsed and I just lay on the floor, a broken man, for a warrior's pride is a powerful emotion.

Alone and in pain, I realised no one knew I was there; I could bleed to death and no one would be any the wiser. I was determined to not go out like that so, finding more strength from deep down in my soul, I pushed past the pain and stood. I was hobbling again, but that was better than letting the pain beat me.

I limped around, and finally my leg seemed to stop bleeding. I then heard an eerie sound pierce the air; it was a blood-curdling scream. With no idea where or who it came from, I finally found a way out of the room and came across a large hallway lit by old-fashioned candles.

It had many doors leading off it and the main door was slightly ajar. Knowing even if there was someone in pain I couldn't help, due to my own injury, regretting the decision, I guiltily hobbled to the door.

I reached the door, and pushed it, and slowly made my way out of the building and down the stone path. Every step was causing intense pain, but I was a warrior and didn't care, as I was determined to kill whoever or whatever had ambushed me and for that I needed to find them.

I could see that I was now actually making my way slowly through a cemetery. I saw large, imposing gravestones scattered with ivy and some were covered in a red liquid. It was sprayed on the stones in an erratic pattern, and I knew this to be old blood.

Once out of the cemetery, I saw the sun was rising and that a large group of people had gathered in the town square.

Curious, but in too much pain to care, I hobbled around trying to find the dodgy tavern. I had just managed to find it, when two people rushed towards me.

Once they were close enough, I could see Lunar and Serenity, their pale faces and worried expressions told me that I was in trouble. Serenity reached me first, and she ran towards me but then stepped back, as she saw the bite mark which was now inflamed and turning green. She placed her hand on the mark, and I winced as the flesh began to fold back on itself and the mark began healing. Serenity took her time, as I knew she was worried that if she rushed it might not heal. One she knew I was alright, Serenity's mood changed, her face went scarlet and she let loose a torrent of words that included idiot, lunatic, and ended with thank The Magnificent you're ok, and a warm embrace. Then, once she had calmed down, I explained what had happened. Lunar and Serenity told me that once I felt better, they would explore the old manor where I was trapped earlier. Grateful for the help, I let the ladies take an arm each and place it on their shoulders and then they carried me back to the inn. As we entered the building, we thought we were in the wrong place; gone was the dirty, old tavern and in its place was a clean and tidy pub.

The tables were spotless and full of chattering men and women gossiping and shouting and being rowdy. We found an empty table and the ladies helped me onto a stool, then they went to find Mallim. They saw her fur boots near a large, broad fellow.

Thanks, Silver. Now that he was back with us, let this ember mistress carry on the story. Silver, just sit quietly; do as you're told for once.

We approached the huntress and she seemed distant. Lunar looked at me, pointed to Mallim's boots and we saw an unusual stain; it looked like blood. My curiosity was piqued so, as she ignored us once more and ran upstairs, we followed her and saw her enter her room.

We both decided that we needed answers about her mood change then we heard her scream, so I pushed on the door quickly. It opened and, to my surprise, no one was there. We checked the room and saw some strange fur and claw marks by the window. Even more puzzled, we just left and went to our room and gathered our things. We then went to Silver's, got his things and headed back to the table.

When we got there, I checked Silver's wound. It had healed well but a nasty scar now stretched across his leg. After quietly revealing Mallim's vanishing act, we prepared to travel on, so we headed out of the pub and back onto the street. Once outside, we found that the whole town was milling around.

The Slaves and Staff's shop was packed; big, burly men and even greater women were crammed like sardines in a can.

As we had no intention of going into a place with such a weird name, we instead wandered around town and headed down a wide path. After following this path, we arrived outside some locked, iron gates. After inspecting the gates, we saw that they were made of wrought iron. The colour of the gate was evidently at one stage gold, as some of the iron had flecks of that colour. The gate lead to the cemetery I had hobbled through earlier I recognised the same bloodied gravestones.

What surprised us most was that, even though the gate was many years old and rusted in places, the lock was brand new. As the light hit it, the gleam of the silver gilt shimmered in the sun. Now we knew something was going on; why was a new lock put on an old gate? Determined to find out why the gates were closed, Lunar cast a *kcoL nepO* spell, but it was no use. As she targeted the lock and tried to penetrate its mechanism, a lite aura flashed but, within seconds, it had gone. I was watching the spell fail and knowing how magic worked I knew an enchantment had been used on the lock, so I helped Lunar cast a spell. We both used the same spell, *KCOL NEPO*, and as the two spells combined, we heard a huge bang and the lock suddenly exploded sending its smoking pieces in all directions.

Thanks, Serenity. OK, back to me. Hi all, Silver here. I held my sword high and, with the ladies close behind me I opened the gate which creaked loudly.

We all heard a thundering sound and, looking back, saw that the large people who had been happily shopping were now stampeding towards us.

With the help of Serenity and Lunar, I managed to shut the gate. Wanting no more trouble, Serenity used the spell *Golden Tentacles* and tied the gate up. The downside was that it stopped us going through it ourselves, so if we lived long enough, we would have to find another way out of the cemetery.

I walked ahead and led the ladies towards a large, foreboding building. When we reached the door, a faded bronze plate was attached to the wall. I could just make out the words which read "***Bloodstone Manor***". Even though I was quite scared, I didn't show it, so I drew the ladies' attention to the plate. We decided to explore the manor, even if the name sent shivers down our spines. ok, I can see Serenity getting impatient. I better let her take over; don't fancy another lecture. Thanks, Silver, for that glowing handover. Now, let's continue. I knocked on the door using a great gold knocker shaped like a dragon's head. The sound vibrated through my hand and, after getting no response, I pushed the door. To my surprise, it opened and we all entered. I saw Silver turn white as a sheet. I could feel a strange energy coming from the door furthest away and, with my new perception, I knew that Darc magic was being used.

Lunar and I crept towards the door, and Silver stayed a little behind in case something came from the rear. As I pushed the door slightly, I heard a horrible screeching noise and then a familiar voice screamed.

I had made up my mind to confront whatever was behind the door; someone needed my help. I pushed open the door and, with Lunar and Silver at my side, was confronted by a hideous group of monsters. They were an assortment of colours, some were deathly white, others were muddy brown, and they stood at least six foot tall and smelt like rotten eggs. For some reason, the creatures ignored me. They had formed a circle around something in the middle of room and were currently making an awful cacophony of noise.

Hold on, will you? Sorry, Silver wants to take the lead. He definitely is Blade's brother; same impatient streak. Here you go, oh mighty warrior.

I tried to creep towards one of the creatures but, just as I managed to get near it, the pack of monsters stopped shrieking and now the monster I was near turned and opened its mouth. To my horror, I saw that the creature had two rows of canine teeth, like a wolf's, which were pointed and looked very dangerous. I was terrified. I realised that the monsters were the nightmare creatures I had heard stories about, known as Fangir's demons; pure evil that fed on the living and used their long, curved claws and canine teeth to kill and feed.

As I looked over, I saw Lunar and Serenity had their own problems. As the other creatures ran towards them, Lunar cast a *Lite Dome* spell to defend herself, while I saw Serenity had decided to be more offensive, as a huge, flaming arrow headed towards the monsters.

Thanks, Silver. OK, let's see how I helped. Hello adventurers, it's me, Luna again, long time no speak. Let's carry on.

From within my dome, I knew I was safe to help Silver who was now trapped by a Fangir on the far side of the room. I used a spell called *Brave Warrior*. Silver suddenly began to glow blue, that's when I knew the spell had been successful. As he lifted his sword above his head, which now had turned gold, with one strike he sliced the evil creature in two. I could see he was shocked as he looked over, and I saw him fall to the ground. Seeing one its number die, I found that the other creatures ran back towards what they were guarding. I was so pleased when Silver stood back up and, with the spell still in his system, I watched him run towards the circle of demons.

Thanks for the help, Lunar. Now, back to me, the great Silver. As soon as my sword had turned gold, I knew that I had been helped by magic; I could feel it running through my bloodstream, I felt quicker, stronger, and more determined than ever to help my friends.

Thanks to my new power, I became a blur of sword and muscle. I dispatched the other creatures without a single mark on me, and the room was soon covered in their bloody, dismembered corpses. As I got to what the monsters had been guarding, everything fell into place and anger tore through me. There on the floor, bleeding, was Mallim. I recognised her boots and knew she had been the one to knock me out and drag me to Bloodstone Manor. Part of me wanted to leave her there, but as a warrior I knew better. I slowly and carefully picked her up, trailing blood towards the ladies.

Thanks, Silver. I'm glad you didn't let anger cloud your judgment. Hi all, it's me, Serenity. Let's press on.

Seeing Silver dispatch, the beast cheered me up. We had fared well. With my use of magic, I had killed four of the fearsome creatures and, apart from minor wounds, had been relatively unharmed. Lunar and I made our way towards Silver.

After seeing Mallim, we all decided that she was our priority and began to drag her past the bodies and out of the room. Back in the hallway, I offered to stay with Mallim while the other two found help.

Lunar and Silver agreed. As the two left to explore the mansion in case there were any more people that needed help, I waited patiently making sure to keep Mallim safe. It was then I saw my pendant glow, and I turned it around and saw the smiling face of my good friend Zelena. I listened and my heart soared as she told me Blade had survived the Cloaken venom and he was going to meet us.

I couldn't wait to be reunited with my friend who, even though tended to be over friendly towards women, was very loyal and would protect those in danger. Zelena went on to ask where he should meet us, and I told her that he could meet us at Mitra, but that it would be a long journey and he needed to be careful. She promised to relay the information and then the stone went cold. Knowing that we would have to stay in this awful town a while longer, I waited for the others to return. It was a few minutes after my call that Silver and Lunar came back. They explained that after checking the manor no one else was injured, but they did say that they had seen a room filled with corpses and that they wanted to leave the mansion as quick as they could.

So, with Silver carrying Mallim over his shoulder, we headed out of the main door and towards the town. Luckily, it was quiet, with no issues to deal with. As we couldn't go through the gate, I used a spell called *Indiglow*. Soon a huge, purple door appeared, and I chose the inn as our destination. Walking as if in a chain, we cautiously entered through the doorway. Being in the space behind the door was a weird experience; we felt woozy and disorientated as if it was a dream. My body felt light and walking was difficult, as everything was flashing past in random colours. Eventually, the sensation stopped and we arrived safely at the door to our inn, though it took us all a few minutes to gain our composure.

I entered the inn first, followed by the others, and we all headed towards our rooms to wash off the blood and dirt from the fight.

Thanks, Serenity. So now I need to explain what happened when I took Mallim to her room. Hi all, Silver's back in the room. As I walked through the inn door, I saw lots of the bar patrons watching me. Some seemed prepared to fight, and I could hear daggers and knives being unsheathed. Deciding to avoid a disturbance, I made my way to the bar and asked the barman for help to get Mallim upstairs. The barman took a quick glance around the tavern and noticed that the other customers were now preoccupied with a large, drunk man trying to get out of the tavern.

He wasn't keen but did agree to help me. We both made our way up the stairs but, at the top of the stairs, the barman abandoned Mallim and she slumped to the floor. Help is so hard to find, isn't it?

I knew that I couldn't carry her any longer; my back was painful, my arms were numb from all the fighting, and my leg still hurt from my earlier injury, so I had no choice but to use the last of my strength to drag Mallim to the nearest room which was mine. I managed to get her onto the bed and then, when I was done, still fully dressed, I fell to the floor and was soon asleep.

Thanks, Silver. You can rest for a while now; I will carry on. Thanks for everything you did, you really are Blade's brother; he, like you, cares about everyone in his party.
Serenity here. Let's move the story on, shall we?

Brightleaf Day 7

The sun was shining through my moth-eaten curtains, I washed the best I could, changed my clothes and then woke Lunar who did the same. Once we were ready, we headed to Silver's room. After knocking and getting no response, I pushed the door and saw, to my surprise, that instead of Silver being on the bed Mallim was. She did look slightly better than yesterday, she had a bit of colour, but she was still shaking and unconscious.

I checked the room and nearly tripped over Silver, who I found sprawled on the floor fully dressed and snoring. Checking he was alright; I bent down and shook him. As he slowly woke, to my horror, he lunged at me. I fell backwards in shock, angry at being attacked. I stormed out of the room and left him to wake, while Lunar stayed behind.

Once I was more awake, I asked Lunar to leave, as I wanted to get washed. She understood and left me. I got myself cleaned, dressed and ready, not easy in a small room with a sleeping Mallim. I checked on her once more; I was worried and hoped she would be OK. After a good night's sleep, I had come up with an idea. I left my room and made my way downstairs.

I found the ladies at a corner table eating something that I guessed was stew, but I didn't want to know what meat the chef had used. I joined the ladies at the table but noticed the atmosphere was anything but calm, in fact, it was frosty. Not knowing what I had done, I asked Lunar who explained about the attack on Serenity. I tried to apologise for my behaviour, explaining that I was half awake and thought she was a bandit, but she just ignored me and looked at her contact stone that was pure white.

A few hours had gone by and, after the ladies had finished their meals, Serenity had calmed down enough to accept my apology. I was pleased and, when everything was better, I put my idea to the women.

Following my approach, we used Serenity's stone to reconnect with Zelena, and we asked if she knew how to bring someone back from a deep sleep.

Hi all. OK, now it's my turn to speak. Let me introduce myself. I am Zelena Starlight, a powerful sorceress and head of Mirrioa. Here's how I helped out.

After hearing the story and what they had been through, I told them that a special blend of plants could help Mallim and went on to explain that the plants were only available in a private garden that was based in the upper part of Mitra. They seemed confused, so I told them that Mitra had two sections, upper and lower, which was divided by a path that ran underground. With this new information, I left them to it.

OK, all you adventurers stay safe, I'm sure we will speak soon. Back to you, Serenity.

Thanks, Zelena. Now, where were we? Oh yeah, in trouble.

I thanked Zelena and decided that Silver would look after Mallim, and Lunar and I would look for the connecting path. It was then that I remembered about Blade coming to meet us.

Silver promised that if Blade turned up, he would introduce himself, explain the story and tell him where to find us. I wondered how their meeting would go, as Blade had never mentioned a brother. Pushing the thought to one side, we headed back to Bloodstone Manor.

After a short walk, we arrived back at the manor gate, but I remembered we couldn't go any further as the gate was locked tight from my earlier spell and the *Indiglow* spell would need to recharge before it could be used. But being resourceful women, we knew that the creatures must have made another exit, and we began to follow the iron fence that surrounded the grounds.

Sure enough, and after much exploring, we found it, a great big hole had been made by the Fangir's demons. We could see the fence had lumps of smelly fur attached to it, as the hole had gone underneath the fencing. Trying to ignore the rancid smell and dodge between the sharp points in the fence wasn't easy, but we were soon back inside the cemetery.

We then looked for the underground path knowing that it had to be there, as nowhere else in Mitra had such a large amount of dirt. We decided to split up and examine each gravestone which was a very long and tiring task. After checking rows and rows of graves not one held a clue, and we could still not see the doorway.

Lunar told me of a spell that she knew, which was called *Uncover*, that might help us. I saw her take out her staff. Seeing it for the first time up close, it looked beautiful. It was made of Rogue-wood and carved into the head of dragon, and the dragon's eyes held two large, ruby crystals.

She held it into the air and began to chant. I stayed quiet, as Lunar's chant became a calming melody. I could see that her eyes were closed and she was now in a deep trance. As I listened to the song, I felt a disruption on the magical plane. This was a skill that I had been taught since I was young by my mother, who was also a mage, but my sense of magic had been heightened after I had become an ember mistress. Leaving Lunar, I looked for something out of place and soon found it. There was now a glowing symbol on one of the older gravestones and was in the shape of a muscular, godly hand.

I walked towards the gravestone and hesitantly placed my own hand on it, as I did the earth beneath the stone shook and began caving in on itself. Within minutes, I had to step back, as a deep, dark hole had now formed.

I used my *Brightness* spell to illuminate the dark and found a set of well-trodden steps. Not knowing what dangers, we would face; I left the hole and made my way back towards Lunar. I was just in time to catch her, as she began to fall; the spell had taken its toll on her. Knowing that the steps would now be easily accessible, I waited for another hour or so until Lunar was feeling better. Once she was, I showed her to the secret stairs.

I used a lower version of my *Brightness* spell on my own staff. It was ok as a light source, but once at the bottom of the steps, we found ourselves in a long, illuminated passage. Torches hung on the walls and, every so often, a small breeze would enter the passageway. We watched as there would be an occasional flicker while the wind brushed past us. I cancelled my spell to reserve my magic in case I needed it later.

We were pleased the gusts were not much stronger, because if the torches went out, we would be in the dark and completely lost. We walked for what felt like hours, our feet were sore, but soon we came to the end of the passage, as another set of steps led upwards.

We climbed the steps and came up through another hole which resulted in another graveyard, but this one was very different. We now stood on what was a polished marble path which felt smooth under our feet. It was a great change after following a dirty, underground route.

Once we had adjusted to being back in the open, we followed the path. It wound through the whole cemetery and to another big gate. As we admired our surroundings, we saw ornate carvings and large, stone tombs dotted like rows of soldiers. Once we reached the gate, we looked up to the sky and found that the moon was starting to appear. Night was coming fast, and we were completely alone.

I got to the gate first. It was a large, black, hinged gate that was inlaid with gold and stood proudly gleaming in the moonlight. ok. Now, Lunar here. Let me tell you about what happened next and in one word; terrifying.

I felt the breeze again that had been in the tunnels, it was back, but this time it was much stronger and had turned into a bone-chilling wind, we watched in horror as the wind took on an evil, black glow; we knew Darc magic was roaming free. Slowly, and sure enough, the wind took on an eerie shape. It became more stable, and a spectral face appeared, then a body formed, followed by two arms and finally its legs. There in front of us, like some ghostly marionette, stood a soul spirit completely motionless.

Thanks, Lunar. OK, guys, let's see how we got out of this one, back to the story. Serenity, all-round mage at your service.

I decided to back away but, as I turned, I saw another spirit. This one had long, black, flowing hair and wore a tattered dress. It had a face that would have once been beautiful but now was like a mask, pale and cold without a hint of emotion.

I could see like myself, Lunar was terrified. We had never seen these horrible creatures and had only heard rumours of their existence from gossips and friends.

Unsure of how to stop them, I was gripped by fear.

I looked over and Lunar was also unable to move. The spirits began slowly walking towards us. Unbeknown to both of us, the whole graveyard was now filled with these evil creatures. The monsters circled ready to kill us and add us to their number.

As we awaited our fate, a large, bright light exploded near the gate. This new sound filled the graveyard and helped bring me out of my fear-stricken state. I decided it was payback, so I dodged past the evil spirits and went to investigate what had caused the explosion.

The noise had also mesmerised the spirits, who seemed confused. I saw them begin to stumble and bump into each other and only a few remained.

As the light was still bright, I ran to the gate and found it had been blown apart. Bits of it were lying in ruins, some singed, others twisted. Whatever had hit the gate was unyielding.

Within the remains of the gate he stood, my Blade. I recognised him by his smug grin and cheeky wink which, even though annoyed me, I was glad to see, and I ran towards him embracing my friend.

I thanked him and then we both went to help Lunar. As we got back to my friend, the spirits had erected some sort of pedestal and, to my horror, they had chained Lunar to it. Blade and I decided on a plan.

It was a bit reckless but, hey, weren't most plans? While Blade began poking and jabbing at the circle of spirits, they in turn attempted to stop him, which caused the circle to have a gap here and there. It was when one of these gaps appeared that I slipped past and was now in front of the pedestal.

I checked all around it, but it was no use, I couldn't find a weakness or work out its purpose. I saw Blade, meanwhile, was now facing a horde of angry spirits.

Hi all, Blade's back in the room after my absence it was good to be adventuring again, and wasn't it lucky that I was here. I was used to being in the centre of trouble and, luckily for me, I could think on my feet and had kept one more shock bomb in store I had picked these beauty's up from a store on my way to Mitra I highly recommend them. I felt around in my bag until I grasped a medium-sized ball. I took it out and threw it towards the spirits, watching in despair as it passed right through them and rolled towards the pedestal.

I saw the shock bomb slide past Serenity and, as it impacted with the rear of the pedestal, it blew. A loud bang filled the air and a blast of energy erupted which shattered the pedestal while the noise seemed to stun the spirits. Serenity and Lunar had been hit with the energy blast and both lay still, surrounded by broken stones.

I ran towards the two ladies and hoped they would be ok, because them lying still like that made me very worried. Luckily, after a few minutes, they both woke up battered and bruised but alive. To our surprise, the spirits had gone and the graveyard was now still.

We were eager to get away from the place, and I was just about to speak when Serenity's stone began to glow.

Hi all, back to me, Serenity. Thank you, Blade. As you all know, my stone was glowing.

I turned my dragon amulet around and, as I did, I smiled as a familiar face appear within the communication stone. It was Lightning, and she thanked us for our help in destroying the altar, explaining that it was thanks to things like these that Mysi could control the spirits but that once we'd destroyed it the spirits weakened.

She went on to mention about Shadowsville and the curse on the town, and to that break the curse we must find another pedestal which was hidden within a private garden.

Being brilliant as well as beautiful, I connected the dots and knew that if we could find the unique plants and the pedestal, we would free the town; as the saying goes, kill two birds with one stone. After delivering her message, the stone became calm and clear once more.

We all walked out of the cemetery and found ourselves in a larger part of the city. Here, unlike our early view of the city, everything was better. Enormous walled mansions were sprawled around, beautiful shops and boutiques crowded the streets giving the impression that they actually merged into one large store.

Blade knew of Lunar before, as he had helped her with her weapon training, but unlike most princesses he had met, he knew she was different and would need to handle weapons to use in battle, so we walked on, chatting about our experiences. I realised that I felt an unusual connection to Blade. I used to dislike his whole image but now found that I was actually falling for him. Of course, I would never admit that to him yet; imagine the smugness I would receive in return.

Continuing to explore this new part of the city, we finally found what we thought was the private garden we needed but, as we walked towards it, we saw that there were other gardens that all looked the same and we had no idea which one was right.

Hi all, Lunar's back. Let me tell you what happened next.

I decided to try a unique spell known as *Truth Be Told*. This incantation would help whoever was in control of the spell, and I thought about what was needed to go forwards. As my two friends watched in awe, the air around the furthest garden flashed a bright mauve, if only for a few seconds.

I was proud the spell had worked, as it was one of the more unreliable ones in my repertoire.

We made our way to the garden, following a beautiful, carved stone path inlaid with intricate patterns that formed different flowers and animals. It took us all longer than normal, as we stopped to look at the many images. The more we looked, the more detailed each became. When we reached the last stone, it held our gaze; the colourful flower entranced us, its varying petals in bright colours captivated all three of us, but then a bright light appeared and we vanished.

We all awoke to the sound of running water and found ourselves deeper within the garden, next to a large fountain. Nymphs and sprites were carved into the design and water flowed from a large pot that a beautiful Aquatican was holding. Her graceful body, part elemental, part human, was stunning, every curve was full of power, and she looked like she would come to life at any moment.

After making sure that no one was injured, we looked for a way out, but all we could see were very high walls that surrounded the entire garden like a stone barricade.

We listened and heard what sounded like thundering hooves. To our horror, coming straight for us was a large, brown horse. As the horse got closer, we saw a sturdy-looking man, who held in his hand a large axe and we all guessed he wasn't there to welcome us. We were now backed into a corner. We were pressed so hard against the wall, I could feel the stone was rough, as it was rubbing against my back and was very uncomfortable. Once we were trapped, the man stopped his horse and clambered off, and he then made his way to towards us. We felt an aura of power and it was really rather scary. We assumed the guy might be a lord or king, as he was covered in steel armour and carried a metal shield emblazoned with some sort of crest. As we were now trapped, all we could do was watch as the man walked around us sizing us up. He spotted Blade and smiled, took him by the scruff of the neck and dragged him away.

Blade was trying to punch and kick this man to defend himself, but soon he realised that he couldn't escape. Serenity and I both wondered why Blade had been singled out. With nothing else to do and now safe, we began to explore the large garden. Wandering down the path, we found that a load of spectacular plants, in hues of different colours and varying shapes, had been planted.

Time passed slowly. After a while, Blade and the man returned, but Blade now looked different. He wore gleaming armour and carried a pointed helmet under his arm. In his other hand he held his sword, but it was now gleaming; gone were the dents and scrapes from his various battles.

As the man came towards us, he seemed less intimidating now. He starting off by apologising for scaring us and went on to introduce himself as Lord Marc De Casey; he told us he owned this part of Mitra. Serenity and I were still wary but followed him and Blade, as we knew Blade could be trusted. Lord De Casey then led us through the garden and into the house and asked us if we were hungry, then he took us along to his lounge. The décor and furnishings were stunning, and we made ourselves comfortable and settled down to tell him of our adventures so far. Serenity took this time to contact Silver and update him on the situation. Thanks, Lunar, have a break and I will continue. Serenity here. Marc and Blade had both left together and soon came back carrying some warm bread and butter and four goblets of wine on a silver tray. Blade did the gentlemanly thing and offered Lunar and I the tray. After settling down, I sneaked my hand into Blade's which, to my surprise, he accepted. I then explained why we had all come to Marc's mansion and asked about the plants.

Marc told us that he had had a varied collection of the plants growing in the furthest part of the garden, but he could no longer reach them as a large stone object had risen without warning and, since then, every night he could hear unusual noises, like whispers and screams, and he had felt an eerie presence throughout the mansion. Of course, we offered to help and explained, if we could find the source of the problem, we would like to take some plants to help a friend. Very grateful for our support, he agreed and offered us a bedroom each in which to rest until nightfall.

We accepted his offer and, after leading us to our rooms, he bid us all good rest.

Unbeknown to us, while we slept, night crept over the mansion, like a blanket pulled across the sky alight with stars, while underneath the moon many soul spirits appeared, the moonlight making them transparent, and they began their stalking patrol around the mansion ready to kill anything that lived.

After only a few hours of sleep, we all awoke and prepared ourselves to find out what was happening in Marc's Garden.

Blade and Lunar came to my room. We made sure that our weapons and spells were ready and then crept quietly down the stairs and out into the Brightleaf night which was now very cold.

Unknown to us, something was scurrying amongst the shadows, and she definitely wasn't a spirit. Our trio stepped into the grounds and we were immediately set upon. As we saw the spirits heading towards us, I cast a little *Brightness* spell which seemed to delay the evil creatures. Lunar had just enough time to summon a *Lite Dome*, and these both helped boost our defences; every time a spirit tried to get near, my spell blinded it. OK, thanks Serenity. Now let's see what else was lurking in this garden of spirits.

Blade is here. With most of the spirits busy, I managed to sneak around the other side of the building. As I reached the very back of it, I heard a whooshing noise, then felt a quick breeze above my head. Glancing up, I saw a slender silhouette climbing up a long rope. Guessing that she was a thief, I yanked the rope hard hoping to deter her. Unfortunately, I pulled too hard on it, and the silhouette fell on top of me pinning me to the ground. The figure moved quickly away from me, snuck off past the building, melted into the shadows, and vanished. I got myself up and dusted myself down. I was determined to find out who the mysterious woman was, but that was for another time, so I headed back towards the ladies.

When I got to my friends, I saw their spells were fading, and the spirits had begun upping their game. More and more of them began striking the dome, and then I watched in horror as the *Lite Dome* shimmered out of existence, leaving Lunar unsafe and my Serenity's spell dead. I knew I would have to act fast or they would not survive the encounter.

As the last spell faded, the spirits descended upon their prey which now included me, as I couldn't let the ladies down. As their skeletal hands grabbed me, ice ran through my bones and I began to feel weak and sleepy. Suddenly, a great light flooded the area while all the spirits moaned, and I managed to open my eyes and saw the spirits begin to fade.

We all watched on as whole groups of them started spinning and their forms melted back into the wind that the ladies had observed earlier. Within hours, the garden was deathly silent, and our foes had gone. The light was still shining, illuminating the whole garden. With the threat now gone, and getting ourselves back together, we began exploring the garden and decided to split up and search for the pedestal.

We hunted for hours, but had no luck, until I saw it tucked away in the far corner. I called to the others, and we made our way to the pedestal, but this one was slightly different. Once gathered around the pedestal, we were all repelled by a sudden force; our spells and weapons were useless, as we each in turn tried to cause damage to the ugly stone object.

To pass the time, I told them about the female thief. I stopped and explained how she had melted into the shadows. I saw my Serenity give me an 'I know who that is' look, and she went on to explain about the well-known jewel thief called Shadowbelle, but with no proof we couldn't be sure. Out of ideas about how to get to and destroy the pedestal, I saw Serenity go to a corner of the garden. I followed, as she contacted someone called Silver. The voice in the stone reminded me of someone, but it couldn't be them, as they had been killed by an evil witch many years ago. The voice said it would be better talking to Zelena as she was very adept at magic. She thanked him, ended the brief conversation and did just that, ok, Blade thanks. So, I used my stone to get help.

A familiar building popped into view; the temple that had housed my friend. Carefully cutting back some rose stems was Zelena, and she was so engrossed that when I spoke, she was quite startled and dropped the stems. After picking them up, I explained to her the problem. Zelena told us that it sounded as if some sort of device was controlling magic around the protective dome, and she told us to look for a jewel or symbol that was probably sitting atop the pedestal.

Thankful for her help, I closed communication and walked back to my comrades. Then I cast the *Truth be Told* spell which seemed to fail, until I saw Lunar pointing towards the pedestal and we all then saw a faint outline that shimmered within the dome. I knew what to do, so I closed my eyes and concentrated on the pedestal where the light shimmered. As I opened my eyes, I saw a quick flash, and the outline revealed itself to be an eerie-looking, black skull that was connected to the top of the pedestal.

Once the image had come into focus more, I felt the Darc magic as the air around it crackled purple and sent veins of energy around the dome like someone was tracing lines with a tainted pencil.

Thanks, Serenity. Something bad was now happening to me. I, Lunar, will explain. I had never felt such Darc thoughts, they pushed against my mind and body; it felt like I was drowning without water. I suddenly grew very still. I could just make out my friends, but it was like I was just a puppet and someone was pulling my strings and dragging me towards the pedestal. My feet moved quickly, as if I was flying.

I also saw that I was heading towards someone but, without warning, I just bashed them out of the way. Having no idea if they were hurt, soon I had arrived at the pedestal and I just sat in front of it while my head and body ached. I closed my eyes and then I don't remember anything more.

Hello, sorry to interrupt, but I need to introduce myself, as I play a vital role. You may call me Shadowbelle, aka the Midnight Rose I am also the greatest thief in Xexus you could say I got famous for being infamous. Anyway, let's carry on from the shadows of one of the gravestones, I had seen the incident and, knowing that the poor girl was suffering, decided to help her, plus the skull I had glimpsed was unique and would bring me a healthy profit when sold on.

I would not let them find out that I had helped, after all my reputation was built on secrecy. So, I crept around the stones until I found a good attack point. I uncurled my large, long, thin, dark green whip, which I had nicknamed the Tainted Rose, from the folds of my outfit and then, with a large crack, unleashed it. The whip whistled through the air, at lightning speed, and headed towards the dome. To my utter surprise, it actually slid through the dome and connected with the girl's arm. I will be back with you all soon, but let me hand you back to Lunar, as I guess this experience is better told by her. See you all soon, or will I?

I felt myself being pulled in two directions. My mind was filled with sad thoughts, and I kept seeing my friends and family being tortured and killed like a never-ending loop. My vision was hazy, but then I was aware of a sting on my arm and now felt as light as feather; someone was dragging me back to reality. My vision cleared and two blobs slowly came into focus. I saw my two good friends, but I was so tired from my constant mind attack that I only caught a glimpse of them before I had to close my eyes and sleep.

Hello again, told you I would be back. Shadowbelle here, I was pleased. Once the woman was out of danger, I loosened my whip and the woman fell to the ground. The man I had seen earlier and another lady looked worried. I coiled up my whip and moved quickly through the garden. I was now even closer to the pedestal; I could make out its intricate carvings and decided to try and topple the vulgar thing. Knowing a whip wouldn't reach it, I felt around in my outer garment and pulled out a five-pointed, metal star. I took aim and threw it with all my might. The star whizzed through the ether with such speed the air around it grew thinner, and the star struck the dome, unlike my whip. It sliced its way through the dome, weakening it, causing the dome to shatter. I saw the strangers watch as my star, thrown from somewhere, found its mark. As it hit the skull, I heard a sickening crack. The skull then rolled off the top and fell to the ground where, to my surprise, it didn't shatter.

I saw the others looked as surprised as me. Having needed the skull, I decided to show myself and walked slowly out of my hiding place wandering towards them. Unaware whether I was a friend or foe, I saw they were prepared to defend themselves, but I also readied myself, as I wasn't just going to accept them as friends.

We all sized each other up, and the man struck first, but I was much quicker. I leapt out of his way with catlike grace and then, when I was far enough away, I let lose my whip. the weapon struck the warrior hard, as I saw the whip hit his skin, ok that's enough for now. Take care. See you all soon.

All yours, Serenity Lunar and I both tried to use spells, but the thief was too quick and dodged out of our way using her stars as decoys. The thief decided enough was enough, all she wanted was the skull, so while we were busy recovering, she managed to get the skull and vanish. Would we see her again, who knew? And from then on, we all made sure to keep updated about her movements, as the tales of her triumphs were told throughout Xexus. When we were finally feeling better and no longer unsafe, we saw the pedestal was now lifeless; it looked no more dangerous than a stone totem.

Just to make sure it wouldn't cause more trouble; I knew what spell to cast and chose the *Topple* spell. This powerful Terrain spell could weaken buildings as long as they were not protected by magic. As the spell worked, we all watched on as the pedestal began to waver and soon it was no more than a large pile of rubble. As the last piece fell, we all felt a strange feeling of hope, a warm sensation filled our bodies, and we felt rejuvenated.

Brightleaf Day 8

Unbeknown to us morning had broken, and a cloudless blue sky was above us along with a blazing sun. I used my stone to contact Zelena and explain about the spirits and the thief. Before we could mention the destruction of the pedestal, she had already touched on it and told us her friend Mikia, the leader I had previously met with Tarum and Rista, had contacted her to say the city folk from Shadowsville had returned unharmed, and we then began to realise that the power of the pedestal had had a greater influence across Rith than in just one place.

I then contacted Silver and once more relayed the story. He was pleased and said he would see us later. All three of us were grateful for the good news from Shadowsville. After ending our conversation, we made our way back towards Marc's manor house. As we got halfway towards the entrance, Marc was waiting for us. He held a delicious tray of food and drink and was smiling broadly. He explained that a new calm had surrounded his house, and he felt safe once more, not living the edge of some Darc power. Once we had eaten our fill, Marc led us past the rubble pile and towards some more peculiar plants. He grabbed one of each and tied them together in a bunch. He then showed us, and we saw that combined together in this way they looked like his crest.

Thanking Marc for all his hospitality, we took the plants and headed out of his manor and back the tavern.

We managed to arrive back at the tunnel with no further incidents and got to the lower city in time to see the tavern open its doors. We walked inside and up to Silver's room, pushed the door open and noticed his room was empty.

I was worried something had befallen him, then I felt a warm embrace and soon realised that he was well. Blade seemed to go quiet as he watched our embrace and, as the two were introduced, I couldn't shake the feeling of how similar they looked. Their personalities were completely different, but they shared some features and traits, but I kept my observations to myself though was determined to find out if, in fact, they were brothers as I had suspected earlier.

After the introductions had been made, Lunar and I went to our room and packed our things, eager to leave the place and its inhabitants. Silver did the same, but then Blade realised we could not go without first helping Mallim.

Knowing that Lunar had the most experience with plants and, as she was an excellent mage, she offered to help cure Mallim, and I also lent my friend my own contact stone. So, while we others planned our journey, Lunar walked to Silver's room. Thanks, Serenity.

Hi everyone, Lunar here. Back to me lets hope I can do this. when I pushed the door open, I was utterly horrified. Mallim now looked so thin, and I saw blood on her arms and legs and skin under her nails. Surmising that Mallim had been so ill she had been hurting herself while shivering and possibly fitting more than ever, I rushed to her aid and began more detailed observations. Her skin was now as pale as glass, and I tended to Mallim's smaller wounds, while dabbing wet cloths to her head which felt like it was going to explode. The heat was so intense, I had to use magic just to break the fever.

Once Mallim was more settled and had calmed down, I contacted Telim who took me, step by step, through how to make and administer the antidote by using the plants as a salve. I was very impressed by his knowledge, and he also gave me a few new spells to help control my own energy as curing such a deadly virus was draining. After many hours and visits from my friends to check on my progress and bringing me snacks to keep up my energy, I began to see a small change in Mallim. I saw colour return to her face and noticed slight movement from her legs and arms. Slowly, I walked back to my patient and helped however I could.

Thanks to my skilled magic and healing prowess, Mallim was soon a lot better, and at last the huntress opened her eyes and smiled a tired smile, but a smile none the less.

Within in the next few hours, Mallim was well enough to ask about what had happened to her, I told her everything, from the settlers' camp to Silver's capture and finding her with the Fangirs. Mallim filled in the gaps concerning why she was working for Mysi, how she had been controlled by him to lead us into the trap and about her ambush of Silver.

She began weeping and saying over and over again how sorry she was. Having been under an evil spell myself, I understood and, after reassuring her, I called my friends in.

Once our party was gathered around Mallim, she relayed her story. After some deliberation, especially by Silver, our group agreed to forgive her but assured her that if she turned on us again, we would not be so lenient, Mallim agreed and offered to help our cause. She explained about a hazy memory she kept having while she was ill. It involved a giant, winged beast, some sort of island, and the colour green. She apologised that it was not much but said that she was sure it would help our quest. With matters settled in Mitra, and after collecting our provisions, all of us were eager to leave the city. We paid our bill and headed back out on our adventure. Thank you for listening. Now, back to my good friend Serenity, I used my stone to contact Lightning, but it took a few attempts to locate her. Finally, after a long time, I managed to get through to her. When she did answer, Lightning tried to keep it short and said she was in the middle of something big. Every now and then a blue, golden glow flittered into focus, and I knew it was her familiar Shimmer, the breeze sprite who had given Rista her locket, I saw Lightning's face and, to my surprise, she looked worried, but it was only a quick glance because, within minutes, she seemed happy again. After informing her of everything that had befallen us since we had met, including Mallim's vision, we asked for her help.

Lightning told us that Mallim might have seen in her dreams a small, hidden island known as **Muck Foot**. This helped, as we had all worked out that the giant, winged beast was a green dragon, but we still felt apprehensive as none of us had heard of Muck Foot, she went on to say that the small island was far away, on the other side of the Joining, near Mudrift. She explained it would take a month, at least, to get there and that the journey was long and dangerous. I thanked her for the help and information and said goodbye.

Knowing that with Mysi still at large we couldn't risk going to Muck Foot, our hearts sank. Just as we felt all hope to save the great, winged beast was lost, I remembered that Silver, Zelena, and Lunar would be returning to their normal lives and duties. Knowing that our band had friends who might be able to help, I spoke to Silver who agreed to the task, as he was only heading back to Mirrioa anyway. Then I contacted Zelena. After much persuasion, she agreed but, to my surprise, Lunar declined saying that she had been contacted by her mother. This time, the message was genuine, as she could tell by the worried tone in her mother's voice, and that there was great trouble in Volcania, Lunar wouldn't say more and every time I asked, she broke down. Feeling better that we had found a way to help the dragon, the last people to contact were Tarum and Rista. Once I had updated them on the situation, I gave them a brief description and explained I would tell them more when we met face to face.

We agreed to re-form back in Mirrorowood. I knew that to get to Mirrorwood it was quickest to fly. After saying our goodbyes, we left the town of Mitra, and Blade and I followed a path through some uninhabited woodland. I found a few odd animals there but nothing deadly.

Meanwhile, Lunar had contacted me to explain her plan; she would be staying in Mitra with Mallim for a while. The ladies had bonded, and she wanted to find out about the real Mallim, not the fake one. She would then find her own way back to Mirrioa, and she would travel on to Volcania with Silver. They would both go to Mirrioa and prepare themselves to then go to help her mum. She told me that she would let me know when she was safely there, and I was pleased she wouldn't be alone on her journey. Knowing my friends were safe, I felt much better. I then took out my gemstones and placed them on the flat ground. I used the *Reveal* spell and soon my dragons appeared in front of me, ready to help.

I saw Blade's surprised face as, even though he had spent time with Pyre, he had forgotten how powerful Pyre was. Blade soon found out, as Pyre let loose a stray fireball and turned a nearby tree to an ashen mess.

I also remembered that he had never seen Ripple, so I introduced her, explaining how I had obtained her. Knowing that it would be better to use Pyre, I walked towards my friend. My Blade followed and, as Pyre lay as still as possible, we climbed onto the dragon.

I could tell Blade was still not happy at the thought of once again leaving the ground, but I knew he trusted my guidance. The bond between us had altered, and I hoped it would continue to blossom. I was so was excited to be getting back in the air, and after a powerful take-off, we were soon airborne. I then remembered about Ripple. I whistled for her and soon my little girl was flying beside us. As she was still young, I found she was too eager and, after being caught in a powerful updraught, she ended up above us and away into the clouds.

Luckily, Pyre was an excellent flyer and managed to climb up higher, using the currents, quite easily. I glanced back and saw Blade was not happy; at this new height he looked quite ill. Finally, we caught a glimpse of Ripple. I beckoned to her and calmed her down, as I could tell she was very scared being still quite young and inexperienced, but soon both dragons were back on track, I knew that the journey from Mitra to Mirrorwood was very long and, as Ripple wasn't as fast, our journey took much longer though everything was going well.

As it had been so peaceful, I saw Pyre was teaching his younger friend some new techniques. Between them, they were spinning, and rolling, and diving. I was pleased to see Ripple having a bit of fun, and Blade seemed to also prefer the calm breezes high above Rith, Hi all. thanks', Serenity. Let me tell you what happened on our flight. Hello everyone, Blade's back in the room.

I wasn't that keen on all the tricks that the dragons were performing, but I did like the fact that during our flight Serenity and I managed to have a proper conversation. She finally seemed to open up to me and told me all about her life, her mum and, most surprisingly, her dad going missing. She kept it quite short as, not only was she trying to get us to Mirrorwood, she was also keeping an eye on Ripple, and every now and then she would stop and listen to the wind, it was during a quiet period that I plucked up the courage to ask her how she felt about me. After our few tender moments, I dreaded her answer but, as my life depended on it, I needed to know.

ok, back to you, my friend. After my dangerous question, how did you feel? I was shocked by his admission. I cared a great deal about him, but love was a very hard thing to accept; it could alter not just our lives but the lives of those around us. Rather than give an answer before I was ready, I found a fair solution and told him that until our journey was over, I couldn't make a decision. After my admission, I didn't know what to expect, but what happened next shocked me to the core.

Suddenly, Blade's hand slipped from my waist, which he had been holding like on our last flight, and he fell off my steed and down into the clouds below. I immediately turned Pyre around and, even though I knew it would take us even longer now, I began searching for him. I had immense trouble concentrating and once or twice nearly fell off as well. Luckily, Pyre was a skilled flyer and helped steady me.

While searching, I had also lost sight of Ripple. I whistled for her, and she appeared from behind a cumulus formation. I could sense she was proud and wondered why. As she got nearer to me, I saw something in her talon. Thinking it was a bird, I smiled. When Ripple was close enough to inspect the prize, my fear subsided about my missing friend; he was the prize in her talon. My little girl had managed to grab the warrior by his armour. I saw that Blade was badly scratched but, apart from that, he seemed OK. I then gently guided and coaxed Ripple to my side, as I could see her begin to falter with the extra weight, and petted her on her snout.

Ripple flew next to Pyre, and I helped grab Blade who was clearly embarrassed by the situation, as he was bright red. I helped him hold on to my waist again, much tighter than before, and I hoped that my answer wasn't the reason that he'd fallen, as guilt consumed me. Thankful he was safe, I knew that no matter what our future held, Blade would be part of it. After our incident, I knew I needed to land, not only to check out Blade properly but to give my dragons a rest, especially as we were really not very far from Mirrorwood now.

As I was so busy trying to land, keep an eye on Ripple, and look after Blade, I hit the ground too hard and rolled off Pyre grazing my arms on the loose rocks and then ending up in a thorny bush. I managed to get myself up, but rather than tend to my wounds, I wanted to check on Blade. As we were finally on the ground, Blade got off Pyre and began walking speedily away, so I couldn't check him over. Instead, I made sure Ripple and Pyre were both ok. I was impressed by Ripple's stamina. After making sure my dragons were ok and tending to my own wounds, I transformed my dragons back into jewels and placed one on my pendant and one in my pocket, then raced after Blade., on my way, I stopped to contact Tarum and Rista using my stone. Once I had updated them on our journey, we agreed a place to meet, but I made sure not to admit to my conversation with Blade. I didn't want to admit to anyone how I felt about him just yet, as the incident had really rattled me emotionally and physically, I followed a rough path that led through some very thick forest. I heard lots of creatures; hooting owls, the howling of beasts, and every now and then something would move but then it was gone. After my run-in with the Cloaken, I upped my pace. Soon I was out of the woods and standing in front of the large temple having reached it this time from a different direction. Its beauty was still apparent straight away, even from this approach. Carved out of the purest marble, it had large, ornate, stained-glass windows. As the moonlight hit them, the images sprang to life, their colour became even more vivid, and I was quite worried as most of the pictures were of the many beasts that roamed the lands.

On closer inspection, I also saw, within the marble, golden veins of spiderwebbing across the building. I walked nearer to this entrance, and that's when I saw two large statues on either side of the door to the temple. Each one was different. One was a large, muscular man wearing a crown and he was holding a large staff. The other was a beautiful maiden with long, flowing hair and in her arms, she cradled a child.

Dragging myself away, I made my way out of the cold and stepped into the temple. Once inside, I saw it had been lit up, as dotted around the room were a lot of tall candelabra each holding seven candles of different colours. The huge statue in the centre of the chamber was of The Magnificent, showing him as a noble man covered in a long robe. He wore a golden crown and carried a large sphere in his hands. Wandering towards the statue, I was overwhelmed by its beauty. Even though it was only a replica of our god, I could feel its commanding presence. Deciding to look around and see what else I could find; I saw something tucked away further in the temple. I found some smaller statues and, to my surprise, one was just a base with no sculpture upon it. I could just make out the singed lettering, and it read "*oodvin*". Ignoring the weird word, I carried on exploring the temple. I then found a familiar statue; it was my friend Lightning and she was in a battle pose.

ok, after retelling that I'm tired now and need to rest. Tarum, it's over to you.

Rista and I had not reached the temple yet, as we had just had contact from Telim about Magna's condition. We had spoken to him on a previous occasion. It had been Serenity who had told me about Telim, and he had contacted me to keep us up to date. Telim went on to say Magna was now stable, but he wouldn't be able to fight for at least another few months. We both told Telim to tell Magna to get better, that we understood, and to confirm to him that he hadn't let us down.

The other reason we hadn't reached the temple was that we were staying in Mirrorwood itself, at a little wood cabin we had been offered by a local woodsman. The cabin was beautiful, as it was situated a long way from the temple, at least half a day, and it was hidden in some dense woodland, after a quick rest, we began our long trek towards the temple but, as usual, the journey wasn't an easy one. First, we encountered some spikers. These were spiny creatures who loved to attach themselves to passers-by and, using their sharp teeth, pierce the skin and draw blood which they would use to grow stronger. Once we had dispatched them using brute force and magic, I healed our minor wounds. Tired and bitter, we finally got a break and spotted the outline of the temple. We trudged towards it, just as the sun appeared. Morning was upon us, but it now meant that as well as being tired and bitter the sun was roasting us.

Finally, inside the shade of the temple, we felt slightly better. We began searching the temple for Serenity and found her near the statues. We walked towards her and Rista tapped her shoulder. This startled her and she jumped slightly. Guessing she was a bit on edge, as it took a while for her to turn around, finally she did, and we saw how tired her eyes were, that they were also bloodshot, and that her hair was a complete mess, Serenity was covered in cuts and bruises. She hugged Rista, and then me, and told us about her accident, then we all began having a long conversation about everything and nothing. We were just grateful to be alive after our long journeys, ok, back to you, Ember Mistress.

Even though we'd talked, I still had not told them of my conversation with Blade, so they were shocked when he wasn't with me. Tarum left us ladies to look for Blade. I had mentioned that I had seen him head towards a small patch of forest just as we'd arrived, ok, Tarum, let's return to you. Please tell everyone about trying to find the annoyingly handsome warrior.

I left my staff with the ladies but took my bow and arrows, just in case I ran into trouble, then I left the temple and made my way to the forest. It was the colour of the leaves that first caught my attention, as I followed the way through the woods. They weren't the usual mix of greens and browns I was used to but had more of a yellow tinge to them. I hadn't seen any foliage like that anywhere else on my journey.

I was just admiring their beauty when I felt I was being watched. Being an adventurer, I scanned the area around me but saw nothing. Thinking my mind was playing tricks, I ignored it and kept searching for Blade. Unbeknown to me, something was watching. It was when I heard the leaves rustle that I took out my bow and prepared an arrow. I was just about to fire when a stinging sensation hit me. I fell to the floor and began convulsing. Opening my mouth to call for help, not a sound came out only a weird foam, I watched in horror as a reptilian man came out of the trees and now stood over me. He was about six foot tall, his scaly skin was pale green, his eyes were red, and he wore a basic tunic and ripped trousers that matched the leaves perfectly. The creature carried a hollow tube. Every now and then, he would open his mouth and, with a pink forked tongue, taste the air., I had not seen or heard about these creatures in any of my lessons. My mind was hazy, and I couldn't remember a single spell. I tried hard, but every time I thought I had one it seemed to slip away, as if my mind was just a raging river, and nothing stayed in.

Hi all. So I suppose I had better explain my actions and why I'd left Serenity. Blade is back, meanwhile, I was still angry and was in no mood to be found by anyone. Unlike most warriors, I had realised I was actually quite emotional I don't think an unhappy home life helped with that, so after this revelation and trying to figure out why Serenity acted strange, I wandered around the woods looking for somewhere I could unleash my pent-up anger. It was while I was searching, I spotted a great opportunity. There in front of me was some sort of reptilian man bending over its prey. I rushed at the thing and, before it had a chance to turn, I lopped off its head. Its torso fell to ground, blood pooling around it, and the head ended up a few metres away with eyes closed, forked tongue to the side.

I felt better, nothing like a bit of bloodshed to clear a warrior's mind, but then I saw the creature's prey. It turned out to be my good friend, and fellow warrior, Tarum. I quickly felt for a pulse. It was there, but it was slow. Worried for my friend's safety, I began dragging him away from the lizard man's corpse. I discovered some of the blood had spilled on Tarum's cloak, but I had more important things to worry about than how Tarum looked. I managed to drag him back towards the temple, where I left him outside and went to find help. I hated seeing Serenity again, as her answer still confused me, but I knew I must get help, so I ran into the temple and saw Serenity wasn't alone. Without a word or glance at her, I grabbed Rista's arm and led her away.

I could see Serenity was very hurt by my attitude; from her eyes tears flowed down her face. I would explain later and hope that she would forgive me. I forgot Rista wasn't the type to be manhandled. As soon as we had left the temple, she twisted my arm and wriggled out of my grip. I was quite shocked at her strength, but she still followed me, as I explained about Tarum, and we both ran to our friend. What neither of us expected to see was how Tarum had changed; he was no longer hurt and was now standing. I was astounded and just stood open-mouthed like some great fish.

Rista gave me a swift kick; she seemed to be handling it better. Having travelled with Tarum a lot, she must have known he was stronger than people thought. All three of us made our way back to the temple, and it felt good to be reunited with the rest of the party. Heading towards the temple, I began firing questions at Tarum, but he had no answer, explaining the last thing he remembered was falling down after being hit with something. Back at the temple, all three of us made our way to Serenity. I stayed further back. Neither Rista nor Tarum knew why I was so distant from Serenity. When we four came together, we felt something strange. The air around us began to shimmer, and then we felt a fierce ripple that seemed to originate from the floor itself. But instead of the floor, it was the roof that began to crack and, to our amazement, it then opened and what we saw was unbelievable.

I saw Serenity seemed most shocked, and she turned pure white and collapsed to the ground, even though she was already sat down. I could see her face, and the tears fell like raindrops.

Nothing anyone said could cause her to react. I put my anger and hurt to one side and put my arms around her and comforted her. I felt her move her arms to embrace me back, and that's when I knew, no matter whether we were to be lovers or not, we would always be great friends.

I need a moment. Please, Rista, can you take over? Tarum and I were puzzled by our friends' reactions and the weird atmosphere between Blade and Serenity. Putting that to once side, we were more awed by the sight in front of us. We saw that a large, blue dragon was now above us. Every so often, ripples of magic would follow the pattern of their scales making them shine brighter. Its wings were huge, thin membrane held up by pure muscle, and the creature had an air of strength unlike anything we had witnessed. It was then that the dragon flew higher and higher until it rose past the roof.

Leaving Serenity alone to let her get over the shock, we left the temple from the main entrance just in time to see the creature fly further into the distance and away from the temple. Tarum and I knew what to do, and we used a contact stone to call on an old friend.

We got through on our first attempt and connected with Resa. Tarum updated her on everything that had happened to us and asked how she and the village were coping. She sounded drained, but said that, as far as she knew from her contacts, the village had banded together and life had continued as normal except for some older residents that had died from the shock of feeling trapped, though she also mentioned that some people had tried to leave and had been repelled and left dazed.

We told her about the great dragon, and Resa said she had never heard of a dragon that powerful. The only thing she could remember was a story her mum had told her about a few dragons that had been reborn under exceptional circumstances. Tarum then thanked his mentor and we broke contact. We both knew that we needed to end this soon, as we feared for Drake's Cliff and its villagers, after our conversation with Resa, we wondered how and why the dragon had appeared. Then we both headed back to the others. When we got back, we told Blade about our conversation with Resa and tried, once more, to rouse Serenity. We both asked Blade what had caused such a reaction, but he was too emotional himself. We saw he had been crying, something which a warrior shouldn't do, but we ignored his tears determined not to make him feel worse.

It was while we were in the temple that Blade told us about his and Magma's incident when they'd tried to enter Graven Vale Hollow. I saw Tarum had that familiar look, the one where something clicked that he had since he had been a young boy. He, like me, must have realised that Graven Vale Hollow must be Mysi's lair, and he was determined to help his town; he had a lot of friends that needed him. As I had guessed, he told us we needed to go back to Graven Vale Hollow. The news, I guess, wasn't taken well, and we all had different ways of handling it. Tarum wanted to try and sneak into the town, I wanted to attack another city that Mysi held so that it might draw him out, and Blade just wanted to kill anything that got in his way, It was during the ranting that no one noticed Serenity stand up and come towards us, if we had, we would have seen a woman determined to solve the problem, she spoke to each of us in turn and made sure she was heard. She used a tone of voice that sent chills down our spines, and then Serenity took Blade to one side and whispered something in his ear so softly. Whatever she had said made him grin like a madman, Serenity then took out her contact stone and passed it to Blade. He used this to call his healer friend Telim. He asked about Magna and learnt his condition was stable, I'd contacted everyone to update them so some already knew and were very pleased, but he also asked about Telim's wife's whereabouts. Telim explained that a minion of Mysi's had broken into his house and left a lock of his wife's hair and a scale from her dragon Shadow. It was wrapped around a piece of parchment that read: "*I will kill her and her dragon unless you come to my city alone.*"

Telim had no idea how to find this place but made a pact that he would travel the length and breadth of the Joining until he found it. Blade begged him to reconsider, but he was determined. Telim was a proud and loyal man, and Blade was honoured to call him a friend, our group, who had been listening to their conversation, knew that the next place to travel to could be our final one. We agreed to meet Telim later and told him to be careful. Telim said if, for some reason, he did not make it, we were to tell Helen that she was his everything. Determined to pass on the message but hoping we wouldn't have to, we agreed to meet him at the crossroads and then, as it had been a long day, our group went to town to rest. Tarum booked another two rooms, as it was a long way back to the woodsman's cabin and, once settled, we all went to sleep.

Brightleaf Day 9

We all awoke to a glorious day, the sky was vivid blue, the sun shone high above us, and the wind took a steady pace. Once we had prepared for our journey, we were pleased that the day seemed ok, as we knew the destination that awaited us was going to be anything but bright.

ok, guys, thanks for my little spotlight, but please can someone else speak? I'm not that great at storytelling. How about you, Serenity?

I suggested that, to get to the crossroads, we were going to have to endure a long land journey back through previous areas, which would take at least a week, or risk going by air. This would cut our time in half but was very dangerous as, during the day, many predators were present.

Our group discussed the situation for a while and, after many heated debates, agreed the air was best, so we all made our way back to the temple and, after finding a good spot, I conjured up Pyre and Ripple. I knew Ripple was not robust enough to carry passengers and that Pyre could only safely take two people, so now I had a problem. How could we all get to the crossroads?

Mulling over many scenarios, I knew only one would work. Asking the group who should go, Tarum said he would stay with Rista and try to find another way and that I should take Blade. Blade grinned once more and walked towards me. To my surprise, he embraced me and planted a kiss on my cheek. I blushed and watched my friends' smiles; I guessed our secret relationship was out.

ok enough of me. Leave me alone while I stop blushing again. Tarum, it's your story, let's hear it.

I kept thinking of ways we could get to the crossroads. I chatted to Rista about it, and she had many ideas but none seemed practical. We decided magic might be the answer, and I kept trying to think of spells to get from one destination to another but realised that neither of us knew one, so once again we called on one of the people who had helped the team previously.

Serenity's friend Zelena hadn't been expecting our call, she was out doing her rounds as a leader, but she had already spoken to another elf who would take over as leader while she was heading to Muick Foot later on after she had prepared for her long journey. Noticing her stone glowing, she found a quiet spot and then opened communication. After hearing our problem, the sorceress suggested we use my jewel. With it she could create a new spell and transport it from her mind to my staff.

She did say that it wasn't guaranteed, as it was just an idea she had been working on with the help of Lightning. Zelena knew of Lightning, as their paths had previously crossed, but that's another story.

OK, so let's see how Zelena faired.

I began to create a spell in my mind. I chose a combination of lite and breeze magic and soon had a new, one-time use only spell called *Place to Place*. Before I sent it to Tarum's staff, I practised on a blue vase. I cast the spell and it moved from one end of the table to the other, but the results weren't great; the vessel had changed colour during its journey from blue to yellow. Not wanting to see my friends change colour, I tweaked the spell and, after another few failed attempts and lots of broken vases, I managed to move a blue vase from one end of the table to the other with no ill effects.

Tarum had been watching my efforts from within the stone and was very impressed. I told him to remove his jewel and place it on the ground, so he unscrewed it and did as he was told, he was a good mage. Once the jewel was on the floor, it soon had a smoky glaze.

Tarum watched as a swirling vortex slowly appeared and there it stayed. He saw me start to shake, and he knew the spell had taken a lot of my energy. Thanking me, he cautiously picked up his new jewel and placed it on his staff.

Thank you, Zelena, for your help retelling that part of the tale. Now I will continue the story. Hello everyone, it's me, Tarum, again.

I was grateful, but she should have warned me, as something unexpected happened. As I placed the jewel back on my staff, the vortex began to shudder. I dropped the staff in shock and told Rista to take cover, as I knew a surge of power was coming. Sure enough, just as we managed to get to a safe distance, the jewel exploded sending shards of glass in every direction. My heart sank, as I remembered the jewel being a connection to my father as it had been his staff.

Something else happened. No longer encased in glass, the spell entered into my mind. The new power overtook me and a rush of magic ran through my veins. I felt it course through my blood and, as the magic hit my brain once more, I fell to the floor. My head throbbed, and I felt hot then cold. As the spell took hold of my mind, the pain subsided.

There in my mind, ready to be used, was a new ability, eager to try it, I asked Rista to hold my hand. A silver and white light flew from my fingers to hers and began snaking around us.

The silver light moved over our heads and grew into a large dome. We were now trapped in a giant bubble. Panic struck us, as we felt ourselves being drawn closer. The bubble was shrinking causing us to be so close we were nose to nose, something neither of us found pleasant; talk about come close to me. Then, with a loud pop, we vanished taking all our weapons and belongings with us.

ok, let me recover a while from that memory and hand back to Serenity.

I was still in Blade's embrace. I wriggled out of it, and then led him to my mighty steed. My Pyre seemed relaxed. He lay down waiting for his mistress, and after eying up my Blade, I bet he wondered if he was soon to have a new master. Once we were settled, Pyre flew into the air. This time, I had created a magic leash to hold Ripple, so we didn't have a repeat incident. Ripple was not pleased with this new arrangement and kept trying to loosen it, but luckily, she wasn't strong enough yet.

When she finally conceded to wearing the horrible thing, she took flight as well. It started off well, as the currents were with us right up until we left Mirrorwood. The air was starting to get colder, and Blade held tighter to me. He knew that, whether I would accept it or not, I was his. Our journey continued to be pleasant, nothing sinister had happened. The only incident had been when Pyre had got hungry and had begun chasing a giant eagle. This had lost us some time, but I knew my pet had to eat as his journey was a long one.

Our journey took us back across the places we had visited. As we chatted about our various encounters and how we had all survived, a glow filled us. It proved that, no matter what the odds, if you did your best, you could achieve great things.

I will be back soon, hopefully. Tarum has now recovered. Let's join him now.

Rista and I reappeared dazed and tired. We found ourselves at the crossroads and waited by the wooden sign. Knowing that our friends would be a few days, I used my magic to create a large *Lite Dome* to protect us. As I was now more skilled, I also created a comfy place for us to rest, and Rista and I got comfortable. We chatted about our journey so far, and we were still surprised about the dragon that had appeared and why our friends had reacted so badly. We were both determined to find out more, no matter the cost.

Having been waiting for days without any incidents, we finally saw a speck in the sky. Thinking that it was our friends, we began waving. It was Rista who saw the first arrow. As she leapt out of the way, it buried itself into the sign.

Soon we were dodging and batting the arrows away. Rista tried to find out where the arrows were coming from, and that's when she noticed a large group of demons heading from the direction of Graven Vale Hollow. I had also seen the group and began firing off different spells, hoping to hit at least a few of the demons. A couple of my spells did make contact. I watched, as two demons that had been caught by the spell ran away, but the group was coming closer. We could see the beasts' long horns and curved blades as they charged towards us.

Just as Rista and I were weakening, we heard a tremendous roaring noise and felt the air around us sizzle. We just had time to move, as a wave of blazing hot fire headed towards the group. It destroyed everything it touched; trees splintered like toothpicks, the ground below the fire sank and cracked, and still the flowing stream of pure energy made its way to the rampaging horde. It was too late. As the monsters tried to run away, the blazing heat of the fire wiped them out, and all that was left was a few melted swords and blackened ground.

When we knew that we were safe, all we could do was watch the sky. After a while, I saw Pyre emerge, his scales glistening in the sun making it look like he was covered with rubies. I also noticed his jaw was now closed and watched as he flew towards a wider part of the crossroads. Then Rista spotted Ripple; she seemed to be sulking. We could see her head was held low, and she was wearing a silver collar similar to the one Chill had been wearing at Th e Mountain Pass.

How she controlled two dragons is beyond me, but let's hand back to my friend Serenity. Maybe one day I will finally understand her affinity with the great beasts.

Blade and I landed with great skill and were soon back on the ground. We walked towards our friend's hand in hand, and we were both smiling. We were happy and now officially a couple. I appeased Ripple with a jaw rub, then removed the collar. This pleased Ripple and, while flying with my dragons, I had made a hard decision.

I had discussed it with my boyfriend Blade on our long flight, and, after much persuasion he'd agreed, but had told me to only do it if I could cope with the huge loss. Even though I loved my dragons, I couldn't stop them being free. With tears in my eyes, I removed the spell that helped me control them. Pyre would not leave me; he kept nuzzling me and growling softly. I gave him one last pat on his snout, then I turned away. This was harsh, but I hoped to show him I meant it.

Hello all, this is Lightning. Sorry to interrupt Serenity, but I feel it is important to hear how her dragons felt, so for one time only I will allow you to access their memories. A word of warning though, this might bring emotions to your minds, so please stay positive.

Pyre's Mind

I was truly saddened. I loved my mistress. She had saved me and helped me grow, but I knew deep down that the love I had for her would always be there, and I did miss the freedom I'd once had. Determined not to forget my mistress, I kept her fresh in my mind. The places and love she had shown me would remain with me as I grew and had a family of my own.

Ripple's Mind

I was very confused. I loved my mistress and had only been with her a short time but, after chatting to Pyre, I too would keep her in my mind. I had decided to stay with my best friend Pyre for as long as I could. I hoped to learn how to be a better dragon and find my place, even if that was somewhere else?

OK, I hope all you readers are doing fine. Now dry those tears and let's press on. See you all soon. Back to Serenity.

After each said goodbye with a nudge to my head, both dragons took to the sky causing greats winds and lots of damage, deep in my heart, I knew I had done the right thing, but I was torn. I hoped to see my beasts again one day and prayed Ripple would survive, as she was still quite young and inexperienced.

Blade and I re-joined the others. We felt very emotional, worrying if I had done the right thing. We then prepared ourselves for what we were about to do. Once we all felt ready, we headed towards Graven Vale Hollow.

Our group followed the now partly damaged path. Around us was silence; no birdsong, no chattering animals, and every tree that had survived the fiery onslaught was barren.

Knowing that only powerful, Darc magic could cause this, we suddenly all felt very fearful and began doubting our abilities. Our joint fear increased, as we smelt a strange odour and then we saw it. A large funnel of green mist was heading towards us. As it built, we watched in horror while it spread out into smaller versions. The smell was so potent now, we all began gagging. We covered our mouths as best we could without lowering our weapons.

I used my mind to cast a spell which was known as *Clear Air*. Immediately, we all sensed the smell get weaker. As the smell faded, we began to recover and soon we were ready to face this new foe. The smaller funnels began to change, and slowly, scaly legs and arms appeared from either side. We then saw heads appear; they were large, bulbous and covered in warts and sores, Rista told us all that we had come across a group of Poison Peks. These horrible, foul-smelling creatures spread all sorts of nasty stuff and were very magic resilient. She had met them once in The Scragged Copse while training.

Ok, sorry, my boyfriend is getting impatient. He would like to take over. heaven, forbid he waited. Everyone, Blade is in the room.

I was determined to protect my new love, and before anyone could stop me, I had stormed into the group of creatures and was hacking wildly. I saw Rista had been waiting for her chance. While I had unsettled them, she also began attacking with her sword. Soon enough, damage had been done that the creatures' wind defences fell and their bodies were revealed. It was at this moment that I saw our mages strike.

They each fired off attack spells, as the creatures were weakened, and, after a long, hard battle, the Peks were slain.

The attack had happened so quickly, and we were all exhausted after our unwelcome action. We knew that we must continue, so we gathered our stuff and carried on down the path.

As we approached Graven Vale Hollow, I couldn't comprehend what had happened. Where the town used to stand there was a huge hole. All around it, debris was strewn like an explosion had just ripped the town apart. The others and I were devastated, we knew that either we were too late or that we had been led to this location on purpose; neither option was a pleasant one.

Ok, my darling, I feel much better for my heroic input, but I would rather hand back to you.

Just as we walked away, I had flashbacks of what had happened at Mitra and it was then I remembered the *Truth Be Told* spell.

I told everyone to stay quiet and, drawing from my reserves of magic, I cast the spell. It was as the spell took effect that I saw the real Graven Vale Hollow; a large village began to rebuild itself right where the crater had been. I watched as each wall, path and building was put back together brick by brick. It was then that I realised that we had all been tricked by another convincing illusion. I told the others, as you can imagine, they didn't take it well, but I will let Tarum explain.

We were all annoyed, but it was during this time that I saw Serenity had been drained. She was now so fragile; she had fallen to the ground and lay still. I saw her boyfriend run to her aid and begin to try and help. He picked her up and placed her carefully somewhere he hoped was safe. I was now really scared, as I couldn't see the village Serenity had seen. I decided to contact Lightning to ask her advice and took out my stone.

But instead of Lightning's face appearing, my stone changed its perspective. It showed a large building with a sign that read Lightning's Guild, shocked at never seeing a stone do this before, I was puzzled for a while, until I realised that I must revisit the place for the answers I sought; someone was guiding me. It was then I smiled. I hoped it was Mum or Dad but that was probably wishful thinking, as I knew both of them had died many years ago.

I told the group about Lightning's Guild, and we all worked together to set up a makeshift camp using the materials scattered around us. We decided to rotate the watch, and Blade took his position on the edge of the camp while the rest of our group slept, after a quiet night, we began to gather our things and head back to the crossroads; we had a long journey ahead of us.

When we reached our initial destination, we had to traverse back through The Mountain Pass. Our group made our way towards the high mountains and prepared for more danger, as everyone knew that this place was the only way to get to the eastern towns and villages, so it was also a good ambush site, plus it was home to some powerful creatures.

Rista and I were more confident with this terrain, as we had traversed it before, so we led the others. Rather than take the same route as before, I decided to take a risk and walked them all deeper into the mountains. The trail was terrible, sharp stones and scrubby thorns kept catching our feet and every so often small rockfalls would shake the ground, so we made slow progress. When we finally reached the base of the first mountain, we found a small river with a stone bridge crossing it which looked quite unsteady.

Rista suggested that she go first, as she was the lightest. We all agreed so, slowly and carefully, she made her way towards the bridge. I could see she was slightly apprehensive at going further, but while I was thinking that I knew she would push on, she had managed to cross to the other side and she was waving frantically at us, waiting to see if we would be brave enough to cross.

I saw Blade and Serenity decided to pass separately, so they each made their way towards the bridge and slowly began to cross. I could see the bridge weaken; small stones began to creak, as they were both heavier than Rista. They both, however, successfully crossed the bridge.

I really didn't want to try, I had always suffered from vertigo, but I also didn't want to be left behind, so digging deep down into my own inner strength, I slowly made my way to the bridge. I was soon standing on it and gradually made my way over. My progress was slower than the others, as I could feel the bridge weakening beneath my feet.

I was halfway across when the whole bridge shook and began to fall away. I sped up and, just as I reached the other side, the entire bridge collapsed into the river below with a mighty splash. We thanked our guardian that we had all made it.

We all regrouped and carried on down the path as our journey continued. On the turning to Lithania, our party encountered some Boulderin's. These small, rocklike lizards were very aggressive and would roll into a hard ball and chase people away from their lairs. We managed to dodge them but received a few new cuts and bruises as a result.

Once arriving at Lithania, we entered the town and began trekking towards Lightning's Guild. When we arrived in the alley, the shop was closed, the windows were smashed and the place was definitely deserted. We were all confused. Why had we been led there? I wasn't giving up. I had been sent to this place for a reason and was determined to find out why.

I tried the closed door and, with a small push, managed to open it. My group and I walked through the barren shop; gone were the powerful artefacts and weapons that I remembered admiring, we all split up and began searching for any clue that might help us discover a way into Graven Vale Hollow.

It was Rista who made the discovery. While searching, she had found a wooden chest hidden under some old cloth. The chest looked plain but a strange symbol had been engraved into it, on closer examination, the symbol seemed familiar to Rista, then she realised why. She had seen the symbol before, so she asked me to replicate the sprite's head that had been on her sword. Knowing the sword was lost, I decided to use a *Transform* spell and found the perfect item in my bag, the tarnished locket.

As my spell took hold, it reappeared as good as new but transformed into the sprite's head, and Rista used it on the chest. She tried to see if her theory was right, so brought the now brand-new locket directly in contact with the symbol and, as she did this, we all heard the sound of a lock opening. She then removed her locket and pushed the chest lid; it swung open, Inside the chest was a Darc artefact made of oakwood and covered in black gems. Worried, as we found that she had been staring at the thing for ages, I decided to approach her and put my arms around her in a friendly hug. After this, she stopped staring at it. I knew it must have had a spell on it, so I used a bit of cloth that was lying nearby to take the artefact out of the chest, and I wrapped it up and then placed it in my bag.

With the artefact safe, our group now had a new problem. How could we get to Graven Vale Hollow quickly? As expected, it was Serenity who suggested using magic, so we both cast *Last Resort* again, and we all hoped we would arrive at our location, as this spell could be unstable and risky; people had been lost in a void or drowned in a lake. What a great thought, eh?

Our luck held and we all safely arrived outside Graven Vale Hollow and, with the artefact now in our possession, we could finally see the horror awaiting us. The village had been turned into an enormous castle. It had a long walkway that covered the entire top of the castle which was being patrolled by large demons. The gate was made from a giant metal ribcage and was inaccessible, with my race's ability of powerful hearing, I could hear the demons chattering. Unsure of how to enter without causing them to attack, we decided to use stealth instead of strength. Serenity and Blade covered me while I strung my bow and found a good spot just behind a large, barren tree and then, taking aim, I let loose a flurry of arrows that had been imbued with power by Serenity ok, let me tell you about my time away from my friends. While I was helping Tarum, Rista had other ideas

I had, by this time, decided to find another way in. So, after exploring the wall to look for weak spots, to my dismay, there were none, but I noticed that there was a large window on one of the towers, more on that later, I need to hand back to Tarum; something big was happening. See you soon.

The demons began howling in pain, as my magical arrows hit their soft, red flesh. Two of the beasts were severely wounded but, unknown to me, the demons weren't alone. I dodged out of the way as a giant, Darc magic fireball headed towards me. It hit the tree which began melting like an overzealous candle. I felt my skin blister, as some of the flames caught me. I knew what to do, so I rolled on the ground and extinguished the fire using the dirt to smother the flames.

On seeing the fireball and its power, I knew that a deadly, evil witch or wizard was guarding the demons but, being a resourceful elf, I also knew what to do. I took Blade's weapon out of his hand and cast the *Pure Strike* spell. My friend watched as the sword began to grow and silver runes began to form on its blade. Seeing the puzzled look on his face, I explained that his weapon could now sap the energy of any spellcaster, but warned him it could affect both me and Serenity, so he was to make sure that he only used it away from us.

After casting the spell, I looked for Rista, and I wondered where she was.

Back to me then. So, let's carry on the story. Rista's time had come again.

I was still trying to find a way up to the window, when I saw a small hook that years ago would have held a trellis. I used a strong piece of vine that had been in the area and, after a quick hunt, I found a sturdy, short twig to knot to the end so that I could toss it at the hook and hope it would connect. I threw it up towards the hook and luckily my aim was great.

It swung around the hook and I pulled it tight, unsure if it would hold my weight, I carefully climbed up it and I found myself in a large room, there was a little swinging lantern which kept lighting parts of the chamber, on each sway, I could make out large shadows, and it was during one of these times I could see the outline of an unlit torch. Unbeknown to anyone, I could do small amounts of magic but kept this talent hidden. I cast a small fire spell and lit the torch. Let's keep that between us for now, as I did this, the whole room was soon bathed in light which revealed the real horrors of the chamber. I saw large metal chains connected to the walls. I found an old plate of food infested with maggots, they were squirming and squelching feasting on something fleshy, but the worst sight was that of a large area of blood. I gagged at the rancid smell of death in the room just as someone entered.

That someone was a huge, burly man. He was about six foot tall and as broad as an ox. He wore a bloodied shirt, torn trousers, and carried a large, stained axe. Without needing to be a genius, I knew he was an executioner and, by the mean look in his eyes, I was his new victim, he had long, black hair braided into a plait. After his evil look, he raised his weapon and swung it towards me. I was much quicker, and I watched as his axe hit the food slicing the tray in half and scattering the feasting maggots. I was unsure if I could beat this hulk of man, but I knew speed was on my side so I understood that was my best course of action, I headed towards him and then, just as he swung, I would dodge his blows. This carried on for a while until I saw his pace slow. That was when an idea struck me.

I led him towards the window and watched as he used his most powerful swing, after I only just managed to dodge it, the man fell over the maggots and slid across the floor. His head slammed hard against the wall, made a bone-shattering crunch and then he was still, leaving the dead man, I made my way out of the room and found myself in a large, empty corridor.

I saw the main door was a little way in front of me. I could just go, but something told me to keep looking. Knowing that my friends were capable of fighting without me, I explored some more, it was while I was hunting that I realised that this building was well guarded, as a few times I had nearly been spotted by either Darc dwarves or soul spirits. I soon found myself in front of a long staircase that led upwards. I made my way up the stairs as quietly as I could and upon reaching the top, I heard a loud roar coming from one of the upper rooms.

Wanting to help, I slowly made my way towards the loud noise and arrived outside the appropriate door. Putting my ear to the wood, I could hear loud sobbing and then another roar, this one much louder.

Just then the floor began shaking slightly. Knowing that this would probably raise an alarm, I decided it was too risky to rescue whoever was inside. Regretfully, I made my way slowly back downstairs and found my way back to the room with the dead man. I then headed towards the window and climbed back down, but the vine snapped and I plummeted to the ground, my hands were burnt and, as I hit the ground hard, I heard a bone break. Hoping my party would look for me, all I could do was wait and sob in pain, now, back to me. Hello again, hope you're not tired of me by now, it's Tarum.

I tried to lure the spellcaster out by throwing minor spells; making it look like I was a weaker mage. My idea seemed to work, and I watched as a Darc-robed figure took to the air and began firing more fireballs and ice ball's.

Blade and Serenity made sure to avoid these, but one spell did hit Blade's arm. I saw his pace slow and that it had made him woozy. I was impressed as Serenity cast *Rainbow Ricochet* and watched as the spell I favoured hit a demon and trapped it. With only one of the great beasts still standing, our odds seemed more favourable it was during this downtime I found Rista was now missing. let's find her I know knew that my leg was now broken the pain was unbearable and I regretted my action of leaping out of the window as now I couldn't move, as I was doing nothing interesting, let's get back to the battle that was raging on.

Unbeknown to me Tarum was taking charge.

The robed figure decided that it was time to kill us pesky people once and for all and, just as I was about to send a massive blast towards him, I saw him vanish. The explosion crumbled the walkway and the last demon plummeted to its doom.

It was just as Serenity was preparing her most powerful spell that the robed man appeared behind her and grabbed her neck. I tied try to shake the mage off, but he held firm. Serenity then let loose a backwards kick. The man hadn't been expecting this, and he fell back winded, I watched as Blade, even with slow movements, saw his opportunity.

He ran as fast as he was able towards the mage, I made sure I was far enough away as lunged towards him. His aim was superb, and I saw his enchanted blade slide into the man like a warm knife through butter, and I watched with pride. As the mage fell to the ground, his hood fell, and the shock hit us. The man's face was just a skull with scraggly, black hair, my Blade withdrew his sword which had returned to normal. Glad to finally have a bit of rest after more battles, we all gathered our strength, I decided I would look for Rista, so I left Blade and Serenity. who were now enjoying a passionate kiss to celebrate the victory.

Ok, I needed to find Rista, so let's leave the lovebirds.

All that lovey-dovey stuff was great if you had someone, but as I didn't, I left, I hunted around for a while and then saw my dancer friend sprawled on the ground near an open window. I made my way to her and could see the relief on her face at no longer being alone her face was tear stained she was holding her leg. I saw her leg looked strange and, as she wasn't trying to get up, I knew it must be broken but, as her break was quite severe, I had to use a powerful healing spell. Once she felt better, I explained her leg would be still painful but at least now she could walk on it, Rista gave me one of her big hugs then told me about her unexpected encounter and the incident with the loud noise, we carried on chatting while making our way back to the others. When we regrouped, Blade and Serenity were now hand in hand talking quietly. I waited for their conversation to finish.

Rista recounted the same information to the others that she had told me, while we made a plan, but we had no idea that someone else was preparing something special for our group.

We made our way back to the window, and Serenity helped Rista climb the wall using her *Golden Rope* spell rather than the vine that had snapped from before. Rista grabbed the rope, tied it around herself then, using all her strength and acrobatic skill, while ignoring the pain in her leg, began to clamber up the wall. It took a bit longer, because of her leg, but she had soon reached the window and, after going through, tied the rope to a metal hook, the sort people would use to tie something back. Then, one by one, the three of us climbed up and joined her.

Rista led the way past the dead man, warned us about the many guards that were scattered around the castle, and told us to be careful. As quietly as possible, we made our way upstairs. Rista walked towards the room, but the sobbing and howling had gone and silent dread filled her, she watched as Blade and I started hacking away at the door, but the noise alerted a troll and some demons that had been patrolling the first floor. Soon, we were both locked in combat.

I saw the troll now had his back to me, so I tripped it with my staff, and it slumped to the ground with a thud and stayed there. Meanwhile, Blade was fighting off two Fangir's demons. Luckily, through his excellent swordsmanship and having battled them to save Mallim back in Bloodstone Manor, he dispatched them with barely a scratch.

Having slain the monsters and hidden their bodies in an empty room, we both went back to bludgeoning the door our joint efforts paid off , but the sight that greeted us was an unpleasant one, inside the chamber Darc magic tainted everything we mages could make out a purple haze that covered everywhere, including a large bundle of rags and bones that were in the deepest corner of the room.

Our group made our way towards the bundle. As we got nearer, we found it was not a pile of rags it was, in fact, a gaunt woman. Her dress was torn, and we could just make out her emaciated hands that had dried blood all over them. I saw Serenity feel the lady for a pulse. When her face went white, I knew from that expression that if she had a pulse, it was very weak.

Ok, Tarum, I need to handle this. Please let me explain what happened. Hi all, Serenity here.

Terrified, I knew this woman needed serious help, so Tarum and I divided our time. He began minor healing spells while I held the woman's hand to comfort her. The others helped by slowly uncovering her, and it was when the woman was turned on her side that we realised that, like us, she was elven. Her body was bruised and significant cuts and scars dotted it. Her body's open wounds festered and a yellow liquid oozed out, Blade told me, in a low whisper, that he knew who she was, she was called Helen Zek. He told me that he was scared that their first meeting might be their last, While I comfort my guy once more, Rista can you please take over for me?

I was checking the room for anything that might help us. I walked towards a large cloth that had been draped over something in the far corner of the room. As I got nearer, I saw dried blood had pooled underneath it. Dreading what I would find, I still tugged the cloth unleashing a torrent of dust. As the dust cloud subsided and it slid off, what I saw underneath made me feel sick and the imagine would haunt my dreams.

Underneath the cloth, a colossal black dragon had been forced inside a much smaller metal cage. Its weak body was hunched over, its wings held against its body, its once dominant face held no emotion, its eyes held no life and, worst of all, its claws were deeply damaged by a large, metal rope that had dug so far into the poor creature its wrists were red raw. I also saw that some of its scales had been cut from its body and the cut marks were very uneven. Knowing this beast needed help, I walked briskly back to my comrades. As I tried to explain about the trapped dragon, I gagged and a wave of nausea came over me. All I could do was just point towards the far corner and then I threw up, I needed to recover. Serenity, back to you,

our joint effort seemed to be working. Slowly, the lady's wounds began closing and her pulse became quicker. Knowing that it would take time for the woman to properly heal, Tarum said he would stay with the woman and carry on looking after her, as he could see the worry on my face as I looked in the direction Rista had pointed, I grabbed Blade, and together we crossed the room quickly. When we got over there, Blade had to hold me as I saw the poor creature. Having never dealt with healing a dragon with so many injuries, I knew I needed help, so I got Blade to contact a dragon expert using the stone, he did just that and was pleased when the connection was made and my good friend Lunar's face appeared.

He explained about the dragon and saw the emotion in his friend's eyes as he turned the stone towards the captive beast. Lunar was sickened but, as ever, she was determined to help this magnificent dragon, she slowly talked me through the healing, explaining that, as a dragon was very resistant to magic, I would need to push myself past my usual strength and unlock my full power if I stood any chance of helping the mighty beast.

So, slowly and carefully, I began chanting using my healing skills and my family's old knowledge about dragons, my efforts seemed to pay off, and every time I faltered my Blade would spur me on. With both me and Tarum busy, and the others keeping morale up, it was at that point when we heard something, A small, scuttling noise penetrated the air, and in the broken doorway appeared a medium-sized Arania. It was awful, it had eight big eyes, long, hairy legs and a hairy body. It got excited about its potential new snack and began lunging its stinger at us; the poisonous barb could do some serious damage. Blade decided to kill the beast thinking, as he was so much larger, the thing would go down easy. What he didn't know was the Arania was Mysi's familiar and was not alone.

Rista, having recovered her strength, wanted to help, so began to assist Blade with dispatching the beast. Hoping not to incur the wrath of the Icilia, the spirits of justice that we had faced previously, we hoped this creature was not an innocent; if it were, she would take any punishment to save her friends.

My friends stood just out of reach of the thing, and both were soon prepared to attack, but it was then that I saw him. Standing in the doorway, behind the horrible familiar, was Mysi.

Hi all, let's leave the heroes for now and I will take over. Your guardian will speak, so please listen, the evil mage pulsed with power, his Darc wood staff pointed towards the party, and he was grinning like a madman. A negative aura surrounded him which tainted the air, and my heroes began to feel disheartened. How could they kill someone so powerful? He wore battered armour underneath a large, frayed, midnight black robe covered with lots of runes. The friends could just make out his skeletal features. He was a terrible sight, and I could see both Blade and Rista dreaded having to battle him, as they knew that only the two of them would be able to fight, as both Tarum and Serenity couldn't leave halfway through their healing spells or they would stop working.

Ok, I think I have said enough. Let's head back to the heroes. Serenity, it's over to you. See you all soon.

With the healing magic flowing through them, the lady and dragon began to feel better, and the lady began to stir. She tried to push herself up, but she slumped back down. Luckily, I had done what I could for the dragon and, even though I was extremely tired, I went over to help Tarum and the lady. It was lucky I did, as I was there to help Tarum catch her. With my additional help, she soon managed to regain herself and was now standing, slightly woozy but at least upright, she thanked us and, as we had guessed, introduced herself as Helen Zek. With the dragon also feeling better, I made my way back towards the beast and, using my remaining magic skills, tried to destroy the chains.

On seeing this human helping him, the dragon's fight returned. After a while, my magic paid off and, with his remaining effort and my continued determination, the beast was finally out of its cage.

Ok back to me Serenity.

Mysi had sent his pet towards the my friends. we were surprised at the speed of the creature and soon it was upon them. Luckily, I had spotted the ugly thing and, as I had started the healing magic earlier, I could just fire off one last small spell. I cast *Golden Rope*. The Arania was too hungry to take notice of the spell, as the rope took hold of the creature and slowly began to wind around its legs. Soon the beast had fallen on its side and, with its stinger also pinned, it could do no more than hiss menacingly at us. Then we stopped, and we all felt a spike of power. To our horror, we realised that Mysi had just unleashed a powerful spell which was now coming for us, it all happened so quickly. Tarum, please carry on but be quick, as it was an urgent situation.

I was the first to see it; a great, Darc mist was swirling away from Mysi's staff, like some significant tornado. As the spell got closer, I now felt broken, and I couldn't concentrate. Images flashed through my head; death and decay. I saw the land barren, the sky blood red, and my new friends slaughtered were they stood. I turned my head towards Mysi. I could see the sheer delight on his face and knew he had been waiting for this moment when he could control our minds, soon, he would have us enslaved but not for his master's bidding. No, we would be his personal team and would help dethrone Blood Bone so Mysi could rule unmatched.

The world would quake at the sound of his name. What he had not banked on was the aid that we his new playthings, had been getting, but soon he would see. As our guardian gave us power, his face contorted in horror, as one by one he felt us recover. He felt his spell fading, and soon the evil tornado had vanished. As he saw my three friends grow in power, his images began to wane. The evil thoughts he had sent them faded before him and, to his horror, a lot of new images appeared in his own mind from years ago.

I, Lightning, will give you a quick glimpse into the mind of a villain, but be prepared, for what you see may change your whole perspective. You have been warned.

Mysi saw himself as a young boy. He saw his home town, his mother and father smiling and laughing, then he remembered what had happened. he had been snatched away. He could now hear his mother's anguished cries and saw his father try to fight the evil creature who was stealing their son. The image changed once more, and he remembered being taught Darc magic. As he learnt to master it, his old life evaporated and, remembering what he had become, the human emotions that he had been quick to suppress flooded back in one long wave. He felt sick with all the pain and suffering he had caused and, after putting his familiar to sleep, was about to beg the group for forgiveness. As he went to approach them, something happened and he just froze. He felt so very empty.

Ok, back to the story. Are you ready to continue or do you need time to recover? Enough time, let me, your guardian, continue, it was then my heroes all felt it. The whole room filled with purple smoke, and they saw a large, black shadow. As it approached Mysi, they all froze. All they could do was watch as the shadow began to feed off him, siphoning his very life through his open mouth. Mysi became weaker. His robe slipped away revealing his bony hands and legs, his metal armour was crumbling, and they could see the pain on his sad face. Even though he had been their rival, they were disgusted at his demise but knew that whatever had done this to him was too powerful and Darc to currently stop.

The shadow, after feeding, left in a blur, the purple smoke faded, and all that was left of Mysi was a dry husk. Unbeknown to the heroes, the once powerful human wizard had been used, abused, and abandoned. As the purple smoke cleared, our heroes began to move, but everyone was numb. As much as they had wanted to defeat Mysi, they'd never expected this.

But they now had another problem. With Mysi dead, the castle he had created began to shake and rumble. Without its master, the castle was falling away.

All of them were trying to get out of this horrible place. The four friends ran down the stairs followed by Helen and Shadow the dragon. They were soon on the ground and out of the main door just in time, as the remaining parts of the building collapsed. They carried on down the path and saw a large group of monsters, also fleeing, having made their way out of the ribcage gates that had recently been broken.

After the collapse of the castle, Serenity's and Tarum's stones glowed and both answered. Tarum's contact was Resa who told him that the barrier around Drake's Cliff had faded. She also said that, apart from the earlier casualties, everyone in the town was safe. Serenity's person was Mikia. He asked how their journey was going and gave more detail about the townsfolk; they had recently been having nightmares and acting strange. He told her he would keep an eye on it.

The party headed away from Graven Vale Hallow and back towards the crossroads.

They were all exhausted, and the mages powers had been fully depleted, but they were determined to rest somewhere fitting, on arriving back at the crossroads, there, waiting for them, travel weary but unharmed, was Telim Zek. Helen saw him first. She rushed into his arms and hugged him so hard Telim had trouble breathing and he was shocked by how thin his wife had become, but he was just so happy to see his beloved wife he didn't care meanwhile.

without being spotted, Shadow had limped away from the group, his pride and trust in people broken. He was pleased that he had been rescued but would never let himself be attached again, the betrayal of his capture was too raw. He would always respect those who had looked after him but needed time alone to think, Telim asked his wife what had happened to her, and she and the others explained. Helen then looked for her beloved Shadow, but all she found were more of his scales. With no idea where her friend was now, she became upset and ran back into her husband's arms. He led them down a path and into a small temple; the healers there helped those in need without asking questions. A young lady led them to their respective rooms. Tired, depleted, and confused, they all feel into a deep sleep.

Brightleaf Day 10

After their long rest, Serenity explained that their town was now safe to return to, so Helen and Telim gathered their things and began their long journey back to Purestrom.

Telim told them, while he was travelling, he had heard rumours of strange goings-on in Mirrorwood and suggested that they explore the place themselves. He was sure, after their many battles, that they could help in some way. He also told the group that he and Helen would check on Magna and report back. After the group agreed, and with hugs and goodbyes exchanged, Telim and Helen walked, hand in hand, together and away on their long journey back home, determined never to be apart, Tarum contacted Zelena. She told them all how proud she was that they had not only survived their ordeal but had also managed to free the towns under Mysi's grip.

They asked about the rumours, and Zelena told them that her city's people had also heard mutterings. Apparently, a large gathering of dragons was heading towards The Great Spire. Shocked by her revelation, Tarum was now more determined than ever to see what the commotion was all about. Knowing that the only way they could reach Mirrorwood was by air, they were stumped as, with no dragons to fly, how could they travel to the centre of Rith? Ok, everyone, I will leave you now; as a guardian I get very busy. Let's head back to Serenity.

I now regretted more than ever letting my dragons go. It was then that I had an idea. I used my stone to contact Seliza. For a while, nothing happened then a powerful, stern, elven woman with long, dark hair appeared, and she didn't seem happy to have been contacted.

I began speaking and said, "I am sorry to bother you, Your Highness, but we have encountered major trouble. With your daughter's aid, we have managed to free some of the dragons.

"We have also seen Mysi defeated but after hearing mutterings of a large group of dragons heading for The Great Spire. It would be nice if we could find out what is happening but, as I set my dragons free, we have no means of reaching it, and I wondered if you could assist us in this matter?"

The queen pondered my news, and it was quite a while before she returned with an answer. Our group could do nothing else but await her response. Time passed slowly and, eventually, the queen agreed. She told us she would lend us her own dragon, Spellvard, but warned that he had a dangerous temper and would only take them as far as the temple, as he was too large to land on the mountain, I and the others thanked the queen, and then I asked when she would reach us. She told me that it would be at least two days' flying time and asked us to contact Lunar and send her a message. Of course we agreed, so Seliza told us to pass on the following: "There is trouble in the ocean, the gilled ones need help." Confused by the message, I ended our conversation, then Tarum contacted Lunar, who he'd been told all about by his great companions, and my good friend answered.

ok, Tarum, over to you.

I did not recognise anything in the room I saw, it was filled with unique bottles and weird jars. Lunar seemed quite surprised by the message from her mum and suddenly ended the conversation, saying she needed to contact someone else, and the stone went pale once more.

Pleased to at least have a way to get to our next place, we all decided to practise our skills. Serenity and I began a wizard duel, Rista and Blade took turns in attacking and blocking, and we all agreed it was nice to have some time to catch up after our long, trouble-filled journey.

Once we had finished our training, I told them I wanted to head back to Drake's Cliff, as I needed to see for myself that my home was OK.

So, after preparing for our short journey, we soon reached The Scragged Copse. We headed through the Copse gazing at the beautiful landscape around us; plants and trees were full of colour. The season had finally stepped into gear, and all the blooms were wide open showering the Copse with bursts of colour.

Rista knew the Copse well and led us down a different route. She walked us through a deep tunnel of trees, and we came to a large, crystal-clear lake, its waters shimmering. Elegant, female water sprites, a different type of aqua sprite, skimmed across the top of the water then vanished only to reappear further down the large lake. Green and mauve frogs leapt across the lilies croaking loudly. She told us the lake was known locally as **Lake Verna**.

Rista then explained to us that she had only ever seen water sprites there and warned that they might look gentle, but they could bewitch and confuse people who dared venture too near them. Rista also told us that there was another special place deep within the Copse, and she led us away from Lake Verna and down a very overgrown path.

As we reached the end of the path, a large cluster of trees were in front of us. We wondered what was so special about them, when Rista then asked me to fire into the branches. Confused about why, I got into position and then strung my bow, aimed, and fired. To my sheer amazement, the arrow was caught in mid-air by a small, blue impish creature. It then brought the arrow to its lips and ate it. I could hear the wood splinter as the thing chewed. Soon more of the creatures appeared and the whole tree was now bright blue.

Having never seen such a creature before, I asked Rista what it was. She told us the locals called them Barkins. She explained they were a distant relative of the Cloaken but, unlike those ambush hunters, these were gentler souls.

Rista then led us back to a familiar path, explaining that the Copse was full of strange things and even she hadn't discovered everything it held. She also told us that, rumour was, the place was created by The Magnificent himself to make a safe haven for the unique residents of the magical area. It was also rumoured that the lake had a deep pit, and no one had ever discovered its depth.

Once out of the Copse, and after the short journey, we arrived back at the stone bridge hoping not to encounter any more ember beings.

We managed to cross it unharmed and were soon back outside my home town of Drake's Cliff. The gate was now open, the symbol had vanished, and the town was finally accessible but, after entering, I saw that the town seemed a less happy place than when we had left. I could see angry faces and worried people staring at us. I felt quite uneasy and thought maybe I should never have come back.

Our group put away our weapons hoping to calm the townsfolk. As we all walked through, we passed many lodgings, and I could hear whispers from old friends with horrible words like "deserter", "coward", and "troublemaker" being thrown amongst the townsfolk.

I was keen to locate Resa, but as I made my way to her tent, I noticed the sad face of my neighbour Refa. I told the others to wait and then walked towards the old man. As I reached my friend, he fell into my arms sobbing. It was then that I realised that one of the older residents that had died must have been Refa's wife, Ruth, as normally she would be by his side. My own heart broke, the guilt I had been bottling up inside me exploded, and I too sobbed for the hurt I had caused my town and especially Refa. Ruth was one of my greatest friends, her stories and cakes had kept me safe when I was younger.

Seeing me fall apart, I saw Rista walk over to me and, after telling Refa how sorry she was, she led me away. Refa, on seeing my emotion, left his home and headed through the town telling anyone who would listen to realise that it was not my fault that the town had been cursed, it was just fate. I guess he hoped that this would help me gain back some of the town's respect, bless him.

ok, I need time to compose myself after reliving that memory, once I had, to my surprise, when I got to the tent it was empty. I looked around for any sign of Resa, but I only saw a tear-stained letter under a stone on the desk. Reading the letter, it said:

Dearest Tarum,

Please don't fret, I am ok, but have had to leave Drake's Cliff. I can't explain now, but if you would like to find me look for me in Volcania. I have left to visit family.

All my love, Resa.

> *P.S, I knew you would make everything better; you're a strong warrior with a heart as big as the sun itself.*

Touched by her kind words, I picked up the letter and showed the others. They were all shocked that she had left the town, and I saw Rista looked puzzled. I guess, like me, she did not remember Resa ever mentioning any family or Volcania, but she might have done as, I had been busy adventuring and might have forgotten.

It was now quite late, the moon was shining, a blanket of stars had covered the sky, and we all decided to stay in the town. I showed them to my home. It was only big enough for two, but I did have permission to use the training ground, so I helped set up a tent for Serenity and Blade and then, as we were so tired, we all headed for our beds.

I awoke to a bright day, feeling glad to be home, even though some of my old friends still saw me as an outsider. I woke Rista and suggested she buy a new weapon, as most of hers had been broken or lost.

Hi all, Rista here. Like Tarum said, I needed new stuff.

I headed to the local smith where I bought a small, light sword and some light armour. Once equipped, I headed towards Resa's Lea and began to practise. I was in my element with my new skills and, along with my dance agility, I had become quite a formidable warrior.

Serenity and Blade were now also awake and they watched me practise. Blade was impressed by my sword skills and, during my break, he offered to show me some new defensive moves. I happily agreed. Serenity began to tire of watching us go at it hammer and tongs, so she headed into the town and bumped into Tarum.

Thanks, Rista.

Tarum here.

I was heading towards the tavern when Serenity asked if she could join me. Happy for the company, I agreed. Once we had entered the bar all eyes were upon us, but we just ignored the dirty looks and mumbled insults and began a long conversation.

Rista and Blade joined us at the bar sometime later, and we made a plan to head back to Lithania. After collecting our gear and saying goodbye to Refa, we walked through and out of the town back towards the stone bridge. We crossed without any problems and were soon back in the Copse.

Rista showed us a much quicker path and, after making our way back through the beautiful, mystical place, we arrived around midday and found ourselves back at the crossroads, but this time something was different. We found a large wooden stall had popped up just past the crossroads' sign. Making our way towards it, a familiar face appeared behind the wooden counter. There was no forgetting those beautiful hazel eyes full of life, it was Zelena.

She realised how happy Serenity seemed since the last time they had met, and she clocked Blade giving her a kiss and realised why. Zelena explained how she had left the city to her best advisor and had decided to try her hand at being a merchant. Then she told us that she wouldn't be there long but let us browse the stall.

We all bought a few useful items including unique charms for storing magic and a potion made from the blessed orchid. Each of us mages bought one charm, and we all bought a selection of potions, she told our group that she had heard rumours of seven tomes of magic that held all the elemental spells, and that they were scattered throughout the Joining.

ok, guys, Serenity is pulling my arm. I guess she wants to take over, so let's give her a turn before my arm is yanked too hard.

I was intrigued by this news and tried to get more information out of my friend, but she wouldn't say anything else. Once we had all made our purchases, we watched Zelena begin to put away her wares and, after exchanging our goodbyes, we left and headed through the pass and back to Lithania.

As we entered the pass, we saw the sky darken and noticed the wind pick up. Soon little droplets of rain began to fall, we increased our pace, while the storm now gathered speed. Rain started lashing down making our trail even harder, as the mud and rocks became slippery, then the winds tore through our clothes with an icy chill, but the worst was the loud rumbling of thunder. It sounded like a great drum was being banged in the sky along with bright flashes of lightning. A few stray bolts narrowly missed us and ignited some trees in the distance.

Determined to get to safety, we finally reached Lithania just as the moon was rising in the sky.

We made our way through the open gate onto the streets. As we passed through, we could feel something watching us. Feeling a bit uneasy, we made our way back to our usual tavern and tried to book three rooms, but the owner said he had no vacancies as a large group of travellers had occupied the inn. They, had come to see if the rumours of dragons were true.

Disheartened and tired, we decided to head back to the crossroads and see if we could make a camp somewhere. As we left the town, Rista heard footsteps coming up behind her.

Let me explain who was following me. Hi all, Rista here.

I turned around just in time to see a small, red, impish creature trying to steal my bag. I gave it a quick kick and it sailed through the air back into town. Thinking that would be the end of my troubles, I turned to walk away, but the creature had grown much bigger and was now running towards our group swinging a magma spear., I suddenly felt a waft of warm air and turned to see a magma beast charging towards us. I was ready, though, and took out my sword and, as the beast struck, I tried to swing at it, but the sword just bounced off its hard skin. Then I saw it turn its spear towards Rista who dodged just in time, avoiding getting impaled on the flame-covered weapon.

I saw Serenity cast *Aqua Blast* just as Tarum cast *Tidal Rush*. The two spells struck one after the other. The first dowsed the creature in cold water, the second sent a wave of water that hit it so hard it flew backwards and then shrank back into the little imp. Soaked and annoyed, it crawled away.

After defeating the beast, we all headed back to the crossroads. It was now becoming lighter as the sunrise appeared. Serenity seemed pleased. When I asked her why, she explained that, by her reckoning, this was the day that Spellvard was to join us.

She then took out her stone and tried to contact Seliza, but the stone remained blank. Guessing that maybe it was too early, Serenity and I realised that we had not agreed on a location to meet the dragon but, knowing its size, guessed the best place would be the Copse, as it had lots of large landing spots that were often used by its inhabitants.

So, we made the journey, once again, back towards the magnificent forest.

As we entered the Copse, the bright sunlight caused the real beauty of the place to be unleashed. We saw shimmering flower's shaped like bells in a variety of colours, large mushrooms and mosses carpeted the forest floor, but the most beautiful sight was a yellow baby dragon that was trying to stalk an insect. We all watched in awe, as the small creature kept almost getting its prey, but it was just too clumsy and kept falling over. All four of us let out a little chuckle and began to feel happy, much later, Serenity tried again to contact Seliza. This time the connection worked, but a large, bearded man answered instead of the queen.

He asked our business and how we knew the queen. We then explained about Lunar and the queen's promise of help and, on hearing the princess's name, he told us that the queen had left a few days ago to visit a friend. She had mentioned that she would be travelling through Black Wood Bog on her way to Mudrift on royal business.

We now knew where to go, but those of us who had been there before weren't looking forwards to going back to the cursed bog. I led our party back to Lithania and along our usual route. This time, rather than go back into the town, we passed it and headed towards the large cave that connected it to the bog, Serenity had told me about the cave in an earlier message she explained that she had discovered it earlier in her journey.

We walked through the large cave and could hear the chattering and hiss of the many small things that hunted in the confines of the chamber. Passing many mushrooms and fungi, we then waded through a waterlogged section of the cave avoiding some vicious fish that had been looking for food.

Not knowing what to expect once we had come out of the cave, we each prepared for possible encounters. Our mages stored magic in their charms and me and myself and Blade drew our weapons.

All four of us slowly began to work our way through the treacherous bog, trying to ignore the many whispering voices seeking to pull us into the different pools. We trod carefully, as a few times we had almost disturbed some venomous bog vipers or a sleeping bog slush.

After a long walk, we finally arrived at a large, flat section of the bog. It was then that we noticed a huge, black shadow above us. We saw it was a horde of flying bog critters, and they flew over our heads chattering loudly.

Wondering what had caused this sudden exodus, we then saw something in the distance. As it got closer, we realised that it was bigger than anything we had seen so far. Its claws skimmed the tallest trees which ripped off branches that then fell like Broughton leaves.

Then the imposing shadow blotted out the sky, and there above us was a massive, silver dragon. We moved away and watched as the enormous beast prepared to land, but this was easier said than done, as it was so big it kept knocking over trees and its wings sent waves of air swirling around the bog. All around us, we could see the swamp inhabitants trying to avoid the significant winds.

Once the dragon had landed, its unique pattern wasn't pure silver like it had seemed when it had first appeared above us. Its scales were all different shades, from bright white, to mid purple, through to dark silver. They shone like a thousand mirrors catching the light and filled the bog with a golden glow.

We then saw the queen; she was stunning and prepared for battle. She wore gleaming silver armour and had a circlet of jewels atop her regal head. She carried a large, blue staff covered in gold runes. They were in a language that we had never encountered, so what it meant was a mystery.

She descended gracefully from Spellvard and walked towards our group. We all bowed when she approached, and we could see her smile at the respect we had shown her. Seliza told us that she had journeyed with Spellvard to get him used to flying, as he hadn't had a long journey for a long time. She also told us that before we could ride him, we would need to earn Spellvard's respect. Our group could do this by asking for his permission to fly, but if he did not agree then we were on our own.

The three of us were nervous about getting close to the dragon's head, but not Serenity. She just walked bravely up to Spellvard, looked him straight in the eye and asked his permission. She waited a while, but then Spellvard lowered his wing, and she thanked him.

Seeing her do this, I followed suit. This time, Spellvard took a very long time to decide but finally agreed and let down his other wing. Tarum and Blade also asked for permission and, after another long deliberation, he agreed, we all followed Seliza onto the dragon and took our seats. We held on tightly, as we felt Spellvard leave the ground.

Soon we were skimming the clouds and speeding through the sky. Once airborne, we all felt elation at the feel of the wind on our face as Spellvard climbed higher and higher. The rate that we were travelling was immense, and we knew that our dragon dominated the sky as anything that saw it coming ducked away, before we knew it, we had left the bog far behind and saw a temple in the distance. Spellvard had to pull up quick as he'd flown lower than he'd meant to, and Seliza told us to brace ourselves for a bumpy landing. We began to descend, watching the ground get closer, and saw the temple shake as Spellvard landed causing the earth to rumble.

We each stepped off the great beast and, after thanking Seliza and Spellvard, we made our way to the temple. We were just in time as, after letting his temporary passengers off, his mistress and the mighty beast pushed off the ground and flew into the sky and was soon no more than a blip on the horizon.

After getting our bearings and now back on solid ground, we headed past a small temple and back into Shadowsville, which we'd discovered was near The Great Spire.

The path was quite short. We arrived outside the gates and told the guards that we needed to see someone important on urgent business. The gate opened, and a young man, dressed smartly, greeted us and introduced himself as Kai and then asked us to follow him to his dad's house.

We passed many people who cheered and threw flowers. Unlike our last visit to a town, we felt like heroes. After a long walk through the busy town, we all arrived outside an enormous, locked mansion.

Kai took out a little, bronze key and unlocked the gate, then he led our group up a very long, stone path and, after walking us to the door, waved us goodbye and paced off back into town, ok, I have said enough. Tarum you're up.

I checked the door and found a large, gold knocker shaped like a dog's head. I proceeded to knock twice, and the door opened to reveal a tall, thin, bearded man, he asked, in a posh voice, "How may I help you?" My group explained our plight and told him that Mikia was a good friend. It was just as he was going to ignore us and close the door that Mikia emerged carrying a large plate of goodies and ordered his butler aside.

Mikia showed us to a large room. He then offered us some chairs and his plate which was filled with warm pasties and pot of tea. We gratefully accepted his gift and began to relax. Once we were settled and well fed, he told us that, after we had saved the town, the people had clubbed together and left us a pile of Xens. It wasn't as much as the town had hoped, due to the fact that some of their townsfolk had died and had needed burial costs. He then brought out a small, woven bag and handed it to me. I opened it and poured it out on the table.

Serenity then counted it, and we were overwhelmed that we had at least 300 Xens. I felt bad for taking it, as I knew the town wasn't that well off, but I also didn't want to hurt their feelings.

I filled Mikia in on our long journey. He was mesmerised by the story and kept asking questions. I told him about the rumours of the gathering of dragons. Mikia said he hadn't heard anything but would keep his ears alert for any news.

He offered us his home in which to rest, as we all looked fatigued. He then got his butler to make up four rooms. The butler seemed less than impressed and gave us a stern look, but he took our group anyway we were all glad of the rest, and we all feel asleep quickly, I saw Blade nip into Serenity's room, but kept that to myself; they were a couple after all.

Brightleaf Day 11

We woke up, gathered our belongings and went downstairs where Mikia had laid on a large spread of toast, teacakes, and honey loaf, we thanked him and then tucked in. The leftover food was wrapped in a paper and stored in my bag. Once again, we thanked him for his hospitality, left his mansion and wandered through the streets. The town was now heaving, large stalls had appeared selling all sorts of items. As we walked past the baker's, we could hear an argument going on and guessed some poor assistant was being berated. My friends and I carried on through the town and then left through the gate. After making a short journey, we were back at The Under-Caves.

After our last trip was not very pleasant, we decided to ignore the caves and explore the area further. To our surprise, we then came to a wide bend in a large river and found a reasonably large boat that had been left on the bank. After examining it, we saw that, apart from being a little bit damaged, it was still ok to use, working together, we found some new wood and vines scattered nearby. After repairing the boat as best we could, my party took it in turns to organise where we would all sit and then, stowing our stuff, we were prepared to travel.

Blade and I took the oars and began rowing away from the mouth of the river and further on downstream. The water was very choppy, and every so often we would encounter large shadows that would pass beneath the boat. We could feel the current flowing faster and hear the water churning. We had soon lost control of the oars, and no matter how hard we rowed we couldn't get to the bank. Now we knew the boat was at the mercy of the river; this was not great.

Serenity and I could feel the boat beginning to weaken and, knowing that we still had a long way to go, I cast a *Lite Dome* spell on the vessel and its occupants making sure we survived the rest of journey. I knew the dome would protect us from beasts and spells but not the water.

The boat was now feeling the weight of the water and the spell, and all of us were wet and fed up, as the water splashed again and again. Just as we began to feel the current slow, it happened.

A huge shadow headed towards our group at great speed, causing massive waves to ripple through the river as the boat rocked from side to side. A tail erupted sending a great big wave which hit my dome with such force it shattered. The water pummelled into us throwing my party over the side and into the deep water.

The boat had been torn apart by the impact, and now we were being dragged further and deeper. We all began to spin and swirl at the mercy of the great river. All of us were scared we would drown and then, after another spin, everything went black, we all awoke on hard ground. We were soaking wet but alive, as we adventurers recovered, I dried us all off with some breeze magic. Our luck had held, as we had washed up on a bank next to The Temple of Rith. After a short recovery, and gathering our items that had been scattered on the bank, we walked into the temple and towards Lightning's statue. We all prayed for her help but nothing happened, she didn't appear, and the temple stayed quiet.

Disheartened, we left the temple and headed towards The Great Spire, as it was only a short journey from here. As we got nearer, we felt a rush of air, then saw flashes of colour move across the sky. Serenity held hope that it was the gathering of dragon, The others and I sped up our pace, and soon the looming, legendary mountain came into view. It towered above us imposingly. We couldn't see the top, as walls of rock blocked the view and it was so high.

From this position, we all looked skywards hoping to see the dragons again. Time passed, and the sky was clear; nothing appeared, knowing that all we could do was wait, we settled down and finally relaxed. After a long few hours, we heard it.

A loud chorus of growls and roars filled the air, and then, one by one, dragons of all colours filled the sky.

I saw Serenity beaming with joy, as she noticed two familiar faces amongst the crowd. It was Pyre and Ripple who had grown much larger than when she had set them free.

Also, amongst them was Shadow, his vast bulk was leading the horde. As he flew lower than the rest, we could see the scars left by his capture on his wing muscles. The membrane was slightly torn, but he seemed to fly fine even with his damaged wing. Thank you, Tarum. Now I need to explain more about the next part of the adventure, as I had the best view. Hello, my friends, it is I, Lightning. You can't see it, but I was finally smiling; my adventurers were brilliant.

Each dragon landed on different areas of the mountain. Once they had settled, something spectacular began. Each one, in turn, let out a bellowing growl which shook the mountain sending chunks of rock falling to the ground.

While this was happening, the sky above them changed from light blue to dark grey, the wind built up, and then a peal of thunder crashed causing the heavens to open. Rain began to fall, and sheet lightning covered the grey sky.

Once the bellowing beasts had finished, led by Shadow, each in turn left their roost and flew towards the mountain peak.

While this spectacle was happening, I decided to surprise Tarum. I closed my eyes and tried to connect with him mentally, this skill was another secret of the guardians, and one we used rarely, as people's thoughts were their own. The only other time I had used this technique was when Tarum had fought the midnight bones, soon I connected with Tarum, and he could now hear my words clearly.

I said, "Brilliantly done. You have freed Rith of Mysi's grip, you have proven yourself a hero through your many actions and managed to band a group of loyal friends together. You are now ready to continue your journey as Darcness never rests."

ok, I have other things to do, so let's head back to our hero. Tarum, it's over to you.

After the strange conversation I had just had with Lightning through my mind, such powerful magic still confused me, After her great praise, I was overwhelmed, so I told the rest of my party about Lightning's conversation and, to my surprise, they were all agreed that I was now a powerful hero and a good friend, Just as I was processing this rush of emotion, a large flash of blue light appeared high above us. We could make out a shape, as a large silhouette appeared out of the light.

I saw Serenity hold her breath as the shadow descended. She seemed completely overwhelmed and just stared into the sky, watching the shadow get larger.

Once it was directly above us, I saw why Serenity was so overwhelmed, as during our travels she had told me of Chill's death, but here he was, not only alive but more powerful, and being ridden by Lightning.

The guardian landed, stepped off her beast and introduced her mount to Serenity as Frost Strike. She went on to explain that Chill had proven himself so loyal that she could not see him die, so had found a loophole in her dad's rule. Technically, she could save his soul and body but only in spirit form, so Chill could live on but not as a real dragon more of an apparition that Lightning could call upon.

Sorry to interrupt, Tarum, but I need to explain how this news affected me, so here it is.

I had mixed emotions, as I missed my good friend, but was so happy that he had been spared even if it was in a different form. I then bid them both farewell and watched them take off back into the air and out of sight.

Once Frost Strike had vanished, we were all so intrigued about what was going on at the very top of the mountain.

But to our surprise, one of us would find out. Now seeing as I was the best at dealing with dragons, it should have been me, but no, it was someone I didn't expect it to be, so I sat quietly and pondered, why them? Back to you, chosen one.

I'm so sorry, Serenity. I had no idea I would be chosen. Hello everyone, a very surprised. Tarum here.

After being collected by Pyre and getting over the shock of being chosen, I looked at Serenity. For once she turned away from me, not even smiling. Knowing it should have been her; my self-doubt began to take hold and I suddenly froze.

Now, not wanting to miss anything, I knew I had to stop this. I deserved as much as anyone to be seeing the top of the mountain, so I took a deep breath and confidently let Pyre take me up.

As I got higher and higher, I found it harder to catch my breath, the air was so thin. Soon, I saw the huge top of the mountain in front of me, its spire pointing straight up like some powerful beacon. I now understood why the place was called The Great Spire, directly next to the spire, I saw Frost Strike and Lightning. Her battle gear shone brightly, the staff she carried had a huge silver ball on it, and it was coursing with power. As Pyre brought me closer, I saw Lightning look over at me and smile. Apart from that, she didn't take much notice. I could see her concentration, and I watched as she shouted the word "SPELLVARDEN".

I had no idea what this meant but, once she had said this, her staff glowed even more and a powerful rainbow-coloured light hit the mountaintop, and it began to shake and shudder.

I watched in awe, as the top of the mountain began to glow. I could see Pyre, not knowing what might happen, was worried for my safety. He looked at me and then began to slowly drop back down the mountain. Despite my protests, I was soon back with my party and most of them fired questions at me, I couldn't answer the majority of them so made sure to walk towards Serenity, as I get over the memory of the magic on the mountain, I need to hand back to my great friend Serenity, After my initial jealous moment, I felt bad for ignoring Tarum, so when he came to me, I hugged him and, unlike everyone else, waited to find out what had happened. He began to explain it to me but seemed despondent, explaining that he'd hoped he would see the Sphere of Time but hadn't. Our party all wondered what had happened after the rainbow magic had hit the mountain, something had happened, and what it was you will discover soon, ok, Tarum, back to you.

I felt upset and a failure, I had not found the sphere, had not saved all the dragons, and had no idea what I would do now. I left my friends and, disheartened, I wandered away.

I wasn't alone long. Lightning soon appeared in her mortal disguise next to me. I was shocked but, to reassure me, she explained to me, on our walk back to the others, what had happened after the summit had fallen, it turned out that the sphere had risen to the surface but, fearing its power would be corruptible, her father's hand had appeared and, with all his might, he had thrown it into the air where it had split into four.

She also told me that something very powerful and regal had been released, but she said no more.

I was pleased that I was now aware of what had happened after the event, and I agreed to keep it a secret, knowing it might change my party's attitude towards me, but I still was very disheartened, as I had not seen the artefact, not freed all the dragons and now had nowhere to go or nothing to aim for. I felt broken, Lightning could see how upset I was. She reminded me about all my good deeds and the achievements I had managed throughout my adventure. When I remembered these, I felt much better, and we had talked for so long I was soon back with the others.

Our guardian gave us all a quick hug, and then vanished.

Epilogue

Hi all, so you have followed Tarum and his party. Let's find out what happened after he reunited with them.

Our heroes hugged, proud of what they had all achieved. So back to Tarum, let's see what he is up to now.

A few months later

My party and I arrived back into Drake's Cliff where, this time, we received a great welcome. A large, two-day feast was prepared in our honour by Refa and the remaining townsfolk.

Magna arrived just as the feast was ending. He had a large bag with him filled with trinkets from Telim and Helen. The one that got most response was a large, thick, tattered looking book tied with a frayed ribbon and engraved with intricate detail. On the cover was the symbol for breeze magic. Knowing a lot about magical artefacts, I realised he had found one of the tomes Zelena had mentioned.

I'll now hand over the story to Magna. I'm sure you all want to know more about the breeze tome.

Hi all, I miss everything. Luckily for me, with Telim and Helen back together, they'd made the special antidote to the poison which I needed to keep taking, and here I was, alive and well. Now here's what happened when I rejoined my former party.

I took the tome outside and carefully opened it. As I did, the whole book fell to the ground and slowly faded away to be replaced by a simple, white, hooded cloak which fluttered in the wind. I took it off the ground and ran the material through my finger's. I found it was as smooth as silk.

I removed my own cloak and tried this new one. It fitted perfectly. As I put the hood over my head, I suddenly felt lighter.

Amazed, I realised I had discovered the Featherlike Cloak, a powerful, ancient artefact from a influential mage that I had read about many years ago in my earlier days.

It had once been owned by one of my ancestors from many aeons ago. This cloak could cause flight for a limited time if used. I couldn't believe that the tome was not real and an *Illusion* spell had been cast on it, but at least I had a new cloak, so it wasn't all bad.

OK, back to you, Tarum. Thanks for listening to an old man's part, I now had the bug for adventure and knew that my journey had only just begun. I wanted to explore the rest of Xexus and see what else I could discover, what friends and foes I would meet, and how powerful I could become. I wouldn't have to wait too long.

Prologue

Hello, dear readers, let's tempt you with a teaser of Tarum's next adventure.

Lightning is taking centre stage.

I was just preparing myself to patrol my land; I was dressed in my mortal clothes which made me blend in perfectly as just another citizen, the only giveaway was my aura of grace and power that I exuded, I was just setting off when I saw a blur of colour race towards me. I noticed it was Shimmer, my familiar, who was trying to get my attention. The fae kept flying around me, and then she flew towards my study, I followed. I was proud of the room, it had large bookshelves filled with a selection of my books on the intricate details of Rith, its monsters, its places, and so on. Also, it contained my silver staff inside its gold holder, but my most rewarding item was something I had been given by my father, it was a contact stone, but this one was colossal. It was embedded in a large pedestal decorated with intricate designs and its surface was like a pool of clear water but, like smaller versions, it could change its colour. It was my way of checking in with the other guardians, as each continent was ruled over by one of us.

I knew that one of them must be in trouble, as Shimmer was my other link to them, as the race of fae could speed between continents easily using magic. I tried to contact Finuan, my brother and **Ocearian**'s guardian. I couldn't believe instead who I saw.

Want to know more? Look for:

Chaos Through the Seas
The Adventures of Tarum Mon

As a bonus thank you for buying this book, I have included another story, please enjoy.

Bitter Rivals

Hello everyone. Thanks for following Tarum's story. I, Resa, would like to tell you how Tarum got to be so good at adventures. I have never divulged this information but you needed to know his story, get ready to cast your mind back a long way grab a hot drink and let's begin.

Tarum's Origin Story

It was eighteen years ago when Drake's Cliff was in its prime. Vast fields full of tasty vegetables and wheat grew, the townsfolk felt protected by massive castle walls, and the only entrance into the town was a big, oakwood gate that was well guarded, the single source of water was a stone well. The elves and humans who had settled their loved their peaceful lives.

It was also there that a young, elven woman called Veres, a competent archer and mage, lived with her husband, Tomos. He was a trained healer and warrior who was under the leadership of Marek, the husband and wife were both overjoyed, as they were expecting their first child. To make this news even more significant, Veres' best human friend, Shyra, was also pregnant, so their children would grow together, everything was great except for a thorn in their sides. He was a rival elf known as Medan. He was spiteful and jealous, an all-around poor excuse for an elf and Shyra's husband, Shyra was the only one in the whole village who had respect for her husband, but everyone knew it was respect borne out of fear, as his temper was uncontrollable.

On this day, Tomos had been driving Veres insane fussing around her. She loved that he cared, but she was only pregnant not useless. She told him in a harsh tone that she needed space, so he left to find Marek and ask if he had any tasks, he needed help with, he found Marek in the centre of town and he told him a young girl was dreadfully ill; she had ingested some sort of unusual plant. It would mean he would have to leave the village and travel to Lithania the next day. As it was dangerous, he offered to send someone with him. Grateful for the help, he smiled, but when a certain elf appeared his smile waned.

His support turned out to be Medan. Tomos was very tempted to decline but saw the smug look on the elf's face. He would not give him the satisfaction of walking away, so he thanked Marek and went to gather his things, Tomos walked back to his home and explained to Veres the task he had been asked to complete. Tears began streaming from her eyes, staining her face, and she hugged her husband but understood.

A few minutes later, the door went. Standing at the door was a heavily pregnant Shyra. She smiled sweetly and said she would look after Veres, as Medan was going too, Veres pulled her husband to one side and thank for, thinking of her, but warned him to be on his guard. She didn't trust Medan in the slightest, though his wife cooked them all a hearty meal and then made them lunch for their journey.

Tomos grabbed his sword and sheath, cloak, and then tucked his bronze staff into his cloak belt. The red jewel on his staff shone brightly, Tomos also took some Xens, a bottle of water and his healer's bag which he placed his provisions into. Veres then set up a spare bed for Shyra and then, as it was getting late, both she and Tomos went to bed, in the morning, Tomos kissed his wife goodbye, popped a contact stone into his bag and went to leave his home, but before he could step through the door it flung open. Medan had come to his house to say goodbye to Shyra. The elf barged past Tomos nearly knocking the bag out of his hand. Medan woke his wife and kissed her goodbye, something his heavily pregnant wife could have done without, as she had hardly slept due to their baby kicking throughout the night, angry at the stupid elf, Tomos grabbed Medan and dragged him outside and up the path. When he was far enough away, he ranted about Medan's attitude and said to him that if they had to travel together, they either got along or ignored each other, either was fine by him, before leaving, Tomos checked in with his friend Vilo, another of the elven healers who was also acting as midwife for the couple. He took him to the side and asked him when he thought Veres was due, as his journey would be long and perilous. Vilo explained it could be hours or days, but it would be soon. Torn between the little girl's health and his wife's unborn baby, he now had an awful decision. Should he risk missing the birth of his baby or let the little girl miss out on full healing?

He walked back towards Medan and explained that he couldn't go; his wife was too close to giving birth. She, after all, was his priority, Medan said nothing then went red in the face with anger. Before Tomos could stop him, Medan just lashed out. Tomos felt the salty sting, as his lip began to bleed. Being the bigger man, he walked away leaving Medan to storm out of the village and down the path. Tomos made his way back to Marek, explained the situation and, after the head villager had healed his lip, he agreed that Tomos had made the right decision, and Tomos walked back home, Tomos was just about to give Veres the good news when he felt his stone glow red.

When the stone showed the image, it was Shyra. He could hear his wife panting and knew that she was in labour. He ran back home and flung the door open. Vilo was there keeping her calm, talking her through every pant, and helping the baby come into the world. Tomos was so confused, he felt guilty for leaving the young girl to her illness, angry at being punched, and elated that he would soon be a father, after hours of holding his wife's hand and helping her, he held a beautiful boy in his arms. When Vilo had settled Veres down, Tomos let his wife sleep.

Vilo then asked for the baby's name for his records. Tomos said they had both agreed to call him Tarum Mon; the name was from the old language and meant one to watch, and they would call him Tarum for short.

But in life, nothing is straightforward. A few weeks later, Shyra had also given birth to a baby girl. But as Spyra had been born, Shyra's husband, Medan, was still away and had missed his daughter's birth. She was worried about her husband. When Spyra had been settled, Shyra used her stone to contact him but, to her horror, instead of his handsome face an eerie image appeared which had her weeping tears. She may have feared him but she still was in love with him, and there, on a muddy path, she saw her beloved husband's body, a sleek, silver dagger in his back and his blood pooling around him.

With a newborn baby to care for and grieving for her husband, she fell into despair. Shyra shut herself off from everyone especially her best friend, her husband, and their new boy. When her daughter was old enough, Shyra took her to Vilo and told him to take Spyra somewhere, and if he refused, she would drown her, Vilo saw how haggard she looked and how bitter her tone had become, and he feared it was no threat. After abandoning her baby, she packed up her things and, in the dead of night, left her village. What became of her no one knows. Where did her daughter end up, that's another mystery, along with who had killed her husband and why.

The real story is that of the young boy, whose journey would begin soon, I hope you liked this short delve into Tarum's past and are looking forwards to how this will affect his continuing journey.

Resa signing off. Now a final quote from the author.

Remember, be a shepherd not a sheep, follow your own path and respect yourself.

Thanks for reading. This is the just the start of both my and Tarum's journey. More adventures await.

May the guardian look over you and be there always.

All my love,
Stephen F Black.

Author Bio

Stephen is happily married and lives in Great Britain with his family, being an avid reader and gamer along with his love of powerful stories lead him to write his own

This book is the first in a series and he has more great ideas to come.

Printed in Great Britain
by Amazon